A ONE-TIME THING

KATE HAWTHORNE

E.M. DENNING

A ONE-TIME Thing

KATE HAWTHORNE
& E.M. DENNING

A One-Time Thing
by Kate Hawthorne & E.M. Denning

Copyright © 2025
Kate Hawthorne & E.M. Denning

Edited by | Jordan Buchanan

Paperback Cover Illustration | Rhu - @rhudraws
Cover Design & Typography | Kate Hawthorne
Ebook Cover Design | Kate Hawthorne

DEDICATION

For everyone who has a cartoon on their Hear Me Out cake.

CHAPTER 1
ROWAN

There was a possibility between the job transfer, the cross country move with a surly almost-teenager, and a house that I'd bought sight unseen that I'd bitten off more than I could chew.

Was the opportunity to move and give us a forever home too good to pass up?

Yes.

Was Fisher pissed at me?

Also yes.

I'd tried to convince him that the move wouldn't suck, that it was too much money to pass up. College fund type money. Buying a new house type money. It wasn't a *great* house, but it would be ours. After years of renting, I'd almost given up on the idea of ever owning my own home. But a promotion, a bonus, and a moving allowance later, one of my dreams for us had finally come true.

The town we were moving to was on the outskirts of a place called Sweetwater, and though most of my work was able to be done remotely, the promotion would require me to shift into the office. I wasn't worried about the change because working in person was a lot easier now that Fisher was twelve and more than capable of looking after himself.

"We're almost there." I'd memorized the exact route I had to take into town and through to our neighborhood. The house was a small two-story floorplan with four bedrooms, one and a half bathrooms, and an unkempt yard in the back. The outside was in desperate need of a coat of paint and the inside wasn't much better, but I figured I could do most of the cosmetic stuff myself and save some money.

Fisher had been slumped in the passenger seat with his earbuds firmly planted in his ears all morning. All the better to ignore me with. I'd figured that Fisher would be okay with the move. The kids back home had been cruel to him all through school. First about his red hair, and then some of the kids realized that he didn't have a mom, and well… kids were jerks. But change could be hard on a kid, so despite his frosty attitude, I did my best to cut him some slack.

The street we were going to live on looked like it was from a movie set, with large trees on both sides and the occasional car parked against the curb. It was gorgeous, better than I'd hoped.

Maybe things would turn out okay after all.

"Fisher." I reached across and shook his shoulder. "We're here."

Fisher glanced up from his phone and looked out the window. He pulled his earbuds out and sat up straighter. "Which one is ours?"

"Four-seven-four."

He sneered. "You mean the one with the jungle out front."

I slowed the vehicle to a crawl and eased into the cracked driveway. "It's not that bad." My stomach clenched. Oh, it was *bad*. I only hoped the inside would redeem me somewhat.

"Dad, you could lose a whole herd of goats in that grass." Fisher unbuckled his seatbelt, but made no move to get out of the car. We'd driven ahead of the movers, packing only the essentials into the car with us. It had made for a cramped ride, but we managed.

"It needs to be mowed. I'll call around tomorrow and see if I can get someone here to take care of it."

My original plan had been to make Fisher do it, but one look at the overgrown mess told me that the job was too much for a singular twelve year-old. "Come on, we'll go inside and check it out."

Fisher hopped out of the car and looked around, scanning the neighborhood before heading toward the door.

The street was almost eerily quiet. Somewhere in the distance, a lawnmower whirred to life. A car door down the street slammed and I took my first deep breath since leaving our old home.

Fisher clomped up the steps and stood at the top. He turned back to me and cocked a half-smile. "At least I didn't fall through the porch. But the day is young."

I left our stuff in the car for now. Absolutely not so we could make a quick getaway. The keys had been left in a lockbox hanging on the door knob, and the realtor had emailed me the code when the sale became official. I punched it in and grabbed our keys.

The lock opened smoothly and I exhaled before looking at Fisher. "You ready?"

He gave me a bored look in return. Some days I longed for the little boy he used to be. Almost-teenage-Fisher acted like I was from another planet sometimes. Most of the time. And the move hadn't made things easier.

The door swung open silently and I stepped inside, my lungs filled with oxygen again as I realized the house wasn't as bad as I'd feared. Yeah, it needed new paint and an area rug to cover the worn-out floor until I could get it refinished, and about a million other things, but it was ours. I stepped further into the house. Dust motes floated in the sunbeams that streamed in the windows.

"Don't they believe in curtains?" Fisher stepped in, leaving his shoes on.

"I'll put that on the list of things to get tomorrow." I raked a hand through my red hair, a darker shade than Fisher's. I told him that as he got older his vibrant red hair would probably darken. I wasn't sure he believed me.

"Can I look at my room?" He eyed the stairs that led to the top floor.

The primary was on the main floor. It had an en suite and a walk-in closet. The guest room, which would be my office, was also on the ground floor. Two more bedrooms were upstairs and took up the whole top floor on their own. It was too much house for just the two of us, but Fisher could have one end for his bedroom, and the other room could be where his gaming systems were set up or something.

"Yeah, go on up." I walked through the house and flipped the lights on to make sure the power company had hooked us up. The kitchen cabinets were straight out of the nineties. The sterile, white, DIY kitchen drawers had seen better days. A couple of the cabinets sat open and when I tried to close them, they slowly creeped back open.

Upstairs, I heard Fisher slowly pacing the length of the top floor before his heavy footsteps stormed back down. For the first time in weeks, I saw a real smile on Fisher's face.

"I get the whole top floor?"

"That's the plan."

"Can I paint it any color I want?"

A knot of anxiety loosened at the sight of Fisher's enthusiasm. Being twelve, it might not last long, so I'd take what I could get.

"It's your room." Time would tell if I came to regret those words or not. "Let's get the car unpacked and then we can find a grocery store."

"I have a list." Fisher headed through the house, back toward the front door.

"I was hoping you'd say that."

Fisher had taken an interest in cooking from a young age. By the time he was eight, he was cooking dinner for the two of us with only a little assistance. I insisted on doing things like draining the pasta water or taking heavy dishes out of the oven, but as he grew, so did his independence. Fisher now did most of the cooking for us. I tried to tell him that he didn't have to, but he'd roll his eyes and ignore me.

Emptying the car took several trips. I stared at the pile of bags and boxes in the foyer and let out a sigh. This was just the beginning. Once the movers got here the next day, it would be so much worse. Fisher and I had already moved a few times in the past couple years; once because I found a nicer apartment, once more because that nicer apartment came with a landlord who didn't understand boundaries, and once again because that landlord wanted to renovate.

And, finally, one more time, to our very own house.

It felt like a chapter of our life had officially closed and a new one had begun.

Fisher dug around in one of the boxes and pulled out a framed photo of the three of us—Fisher, myself, and his mother, Lisa. The first thing we unpacked when we got to a new place had always been the picture of the three of us.

"Can we put it in my room?" Fisher asked, clinging to the frame like it was a lifeline.

"Of course you can." I had other pictures, and if I was honest, I didn't need the photo as much as Fisher did. We lost the same person, but our losses were not the same. Lisa had been my best friend, my wife, the mother of my child. But losing your mom was a different kind of pain.

Fisher grabbed a bag and headed upstairs with it and the picture. I gathered the rest of his things and carried them up the stairs for him, setting them on the landing between the two bedrooms. The top floor was going to be perfect for him. All it needed was a coat of paint, some new light fixtures, and the carpet to be taken out, and it would be a great space.

"What room do you want your stuff in?"

Fisher popped out of the room to my right.

"This one." He disappeared behind the door and I carried some of his stuff into the room. The one he'd selected had a small closet with a few hangers left behind on the rod. I was going to ask if Fisher was sure, but Fisher had found a nail in the wall and had already hung his mother's picture, claiming the space.

"You know, Dad, now that we're not renting and we have a yard, we could get a dog."

Reaching out, I ruffled his hair. "Try again in a few weeks once the lawn has been mowed, the walls have been painted, and we're all settled in. We don't even have furniture yet. Besides, you might decide you want a cat."

"Fat chance. I want a dog. A big one."

Fisher had wanted a dog since he could talk, but it was already difficult to be a renter, even without a dog. Adding a pet to the mix would have complicated things a million times over.

"We'll see."

He beamed at me, his whole face lit up like a firework. "That wasn't a no."

"It wasn't a no. It was a *not right now*."

"I can work with that. Come on, I want to hit the grocery store." Fisher put his hands on me and steered me out of the room.

"Gee, who's the adult here?"

"If we're basing the question off of who likes grocery shopping, not you. So do as you're told, Dad."

Fisher and I left the rest of the things we'd unpacked

all heaped up in the middle of the room and climbed back into the car.

"Do me a favor and give me directions to the nearest grocery store," I told him as I started the car. I had a rough idea of where it was, but it would be good for Fisher to learn his way around our new town.

I backed out of the driveway and slowly started up the street.

"Wow, Dad, look at that."

We'd just turned the corner and Fisher pointed at an old car inside of an open garage.. "What kind of car is that?"

"A classic one. I don't know what it's called, though." I caught a glimpse of the neighbor, messy dark hair, tight jeans with holes in the knees, a black, skin-tight shirt, and that was enough for to make my mouth go dry. "Come on, directions, Fisher."

"Right. I mean right as in okay, not take a right. Actually, you'll want to go straight."

Straight indeed.

I tried not to think about the neighbor's ass and the way it looked in those jeans.

CHAPTER 2
GIL

It was a Friday afternoon, the sun setting behind me and casting my garage in a sweltering kind of heat that made it near impossible to keep working. The concrete floor looked painted orange, the rays of the sun reflecting purple and green off a puddle of oil in the corner. My shirt clung to my shoulders and sweat dripped into my eye, everything aligning to tell me it was time to pack it in for the night. I tightened a loose bolt and backed out from beneath the open hood, swiping the back of my hand across my damp forehead.

"You look like you need a beer," my best friend Jack said from his comfortable seat in the far corner of my garage. He finished the last of his beer, crushing the can in his fist before tossing it into the nearby trashcan. He was situated in the last remaining patch of shade in my two-car garage, the old wooden kitchen chair beneath him having seen its fair share of sun over the years. Jack balanced his weight on the back two legs, rocking into the wall to hold himself up.

"Let me guess," I asked with a sigh. "That was the last one?"

"Right-o, bestie."

I unhooked the prop rod and slammed the hood closed. I'd bought my '67 Cougar two years ago, and getting it restored had turned out to be much more of a process than I'd planned. I hadn't given her priority, though, instead spending as much time on my motorcycle as I could manage. Jack liked to tell me I couldn't outpace my problems on the bike, but it didn't stop me from trying. The car was supposed to have been something to focus my attention on after a breakup, and she'd been that and more, which might have been the reason I'd dragged it out for as long as I had.

"You're the one with a car that runs," I reminded him. "Why don't you go get some more?"

"You're the one with the plush job," he said with a grin.

"You make six figures."

"Barely."

Reaching into the back pocket of my worn black jeans for my wallet, I pulled a twenty dollar bill out and waved it in front of his face. He rocked forward onto the front legs of the chair and snatched it out of my hand.

"How about instead of me going to get another six-pack, you clean up and we head out of town for a drink?" Jack proposed, pocketing my money.

"Is this another of your attempts to get me laid?"

He bobbled his head from side to side. "How long has it been?"

"I don't know."

"Don't lie."

I let out a slow exhale, reaching up to trace my finger back and forth across the split scar in the middle of my right eyebrow. The scar was from a bike accident I'd had in my early thirties, the tight skin running from the top of my forehead, over my eye, and down into my cheek. I was lucky, the doctors said. I could have lost the eye entirely, but thanks to the marvels of modern medicine, I'd managed to keep it. My vision was sometimes blurrier on that side than the other, but beyond the scar, there wasn't much physical evidence of the fact I'd almost died alone one night in the middle of a two-lane mountain highway.

"You know how long it's been," I answered, brushing past Jack and heading into the house.

The sound of his laughter followed me inside, but I didn't bother paying him any attention as I stretched my arms behind me to ruck up my shirt. The dirty cotton clung to my skin as I pulled it up and over my head. Jack detoured into my kitchen as I continued on into the bedroom. Tossing my shirt into the hamper, I popped open the fly of my jeans while I toed off my work boots.

"I take it you're coming out, then?" he called down the hallway at me.

I kicked my shoes against the wall and shoved my pants down to my ankles. "It feels like a better use of my money."

"I don't want to fuck you, Gil, but you're objectively hot," he shouted back. "Two years is too long. For you and for anyone who wants to see you naked."

"I don't think that's as flattering as you think it is," I called to him.

"Just take a shower and put on something presentable."

I closed my bedroom door with a little more force than was rightly necessary, even though it was nowhere near enough of a divider to drown out the sound of Jack's laughter. I hated the man as much as I loved him, but I'd never let on to the second part or it would go to his head and I'd never hear the end of it. I'd known Jack for seven years, and I'd nearly lost him two years earlier on account of the fact he was the brother of the last man I slept with.

I got along better with Jack than I ever did with Philip, and when the romance between Philip and me finally snuffed itself out, I worried I'd lose not just my partner, but the man who'd become my closest friend. Thankfully, after a rocky couple months of navigating separating two lives that had become desperately tangled, everything settled and there was Jack again, as friendly and kind to me as he'd ever been. It had been months, almost twenty of them, since we'd even mentioned his brother. It was sort of a silent agreement between us. Our own kind of don't ask, don't tell. I wouldn't ask what Philip was up to, and he wouldn't offer. I also knew he kept our friendship close to his chest, giving his brother the same silence about me and my life.

Climbing into the shower, I scrubbed the oil off my forearms, knowing there wasn't anything to be done about the state of my fingernails. I washed my body, shampooed my hair, then rinsed all the suds away and stepped back onto the mat. Jack had told me to make myself presentable, but Sweetwater was a large and boring place, and there wasn't anyone around that I wanted to impress. As much as it killed him, I didn't want to cruise. I wasn't interested in a random hookup with someone I'd run into a week later in the produce aisle. I wasn't interested in a relationship either. Philip had sucked that right out of me, along with a lifetime of cum, but that didn't matter much anymore. There was less opportunity to get hurt if I kept my dick in my pants and everyone at arm's length.

Something crashed in my kitchen, and I knew I'd left Jack unattended for long enough. I pulled on the cleanest pair of jeans I could find and a black t-shirt that had seen better days. It was so faded it was nearly gray, threadbare around the sleeves and worn in the middle of the chest. It clung to my still damp skin, so I dried as much of my shoulder-length hair as I could manage before heading out of my bedroom.

I found Jack in the kitchen, grinning and yanking a drawer open. He slammed it closed, silverware rattling, then repeated the process once more for good measure.

"You're insufferable," I told him, shoving my hair out of my face.

"It worked," he said with a smile. "I was bored and now here you are to entertain me."

"Just take the twenty and fuck off," I said.

He shook his head. "That's absolutely not happening. We're going to Ridgecrest tonight whether you like it or not."

"I don't like it," I said.

"Cool. I'll drive. All you have to do is figure out how to talk to people."

"I don't enjoy talking to people."

"That's why no one wants to fuck you," he teased.

"I find sex is better without conversation."

That wasn't entirely true, but…

"You don't find sex at all." Jack gave my silverware drawer one last open and close, then he clapped me on the back and headed for the door to the garage. His Audi was parked on the street, and I obediently followed after him. Even if I had no intention of trying to get laid, I was looking forward to going out with him. I'd never let on, though. His ego would get uncontrollable if he knew how much I truly enjoyed his company.

The fact of the matter was that, on the whole, I didn't enjoy people. I wasn't friendly and I was far from social. If it wasn't the off-putting nature of my facial scar, it was the ice green of my eyes or the flash of white in the front of my hairline that I'd developed at nineteen. If it wasn't any of those things, it was my height—nearing six-foot-four—or my attitude…the constant frown that marred my features far worse than the scar ever could.

The fact that Philip had taken a chance on me was a miracle in and of itself. Much like my friendship with Jack, I'd been resistant to him at first too, but all it took was perseverance to wear me down. I think, though it was another thing I'd never admit, it meant a lot to me that both of them had tried. In the end, Jack was the one who'd put the most work in, and I put more value in our friendship than I ever had in my romantic inclinations with Philip.

"If I didn't know you as well as I do, I'd suggest you start therapy," I said, pulling open the passenger door of Jack's car and sliding down into the seat. Even though I'd just showered, I didn't even feel anywhere close to clean enough to be in a car as nice as his, but he was the one who'd wanted to go out, so he could get it detailed later if I left any grease or oil behind.

"I'll have you know I'm in therapy, thank you very much." He closed the door on me and went around to the driver's side.

I scrunched my nose, angling my face toward him. "Since when?"

"Since…" Jack trailed off, his mouth turning down into a frown. "A few months ago? I honestly don't remember."

"Why didn't you say anything?"

"I didn't want you to make a big deal out of it." He shrugged. "Besides, the doctor says it's just mild depression, nothing to worry about."

I pulled my lower lip between my teeth, tracing my tongue over the chapped skin. "I was just teasing about you needing therapy, but you know you can talk to me about anything, right?"

"I know, but…not this." Jack gave me half a smile and turned his attention back to the road. "I'm fine, but let's just say going out together is as good for me as it will be for you."

"So it's horrible," I deadpanned.

"Yes," he nodded somberly, taking the next turn a little faster than necessary.

My body slid into the passenger door hard enough to push a grunt out of my lungs, which only made Jack laugh. On the straightaway, he gunned it, and I unrolled my window to enjoy the breeze against my cheeks. Connecting my phone to the radio before Jack could protest, I cranked up the volume on a late-nineties punk rock playlist and closed my eyes, letting the music carry us into whatever trouble Jack was ready to find.

Maybe he was right.

Maybe getting laid wouldn't be such a bad idea after all.

CHAPTER 3
ROWAN

f the four-foot-tall grass didn't kill me, the sun was going to. I'd been attempting to get the back yard in shape all weekend so Fisher could have a space at home to hang out. It wasn't a huge yard, but it had been left to its own devices for years. The result was that it now looked like an overgrown weed patch. Eventually I'd have to fix the fence, but first I'd have to *get* to it.

Currently the sun-bleached boards were half hidden by the unruly grass patch that used to be a lawn. Earlier, I'd tried to tackle it, but I should have known you couldn't cut waist-high vegetation with a push mower.

The phone in the back pocket of my shorts vibrated and I killed the weed whacker and mopped the sweat off my face with the bottom of my shirt.

"Hey, Eric." I dropped down onto a chair that I'd brought outside and set up in the shade of the house by the back door.

"Hey, traitor. How's Sweetwater? Miss me yet?"

"It's great." I tried to regulate my breathing so Eric

wouldn't be able to hear me huffing and puffing. "And of course I miss you."

"Of course you do. How's the house coming? Is it a palace yet?"

I snorted. "Hardly. I'm taming the jungle in the back, then I'll work on the front yard before taking on the inside."

"Show me around." Eric said. "Let me see what you left me for."

"You're so dramatic. I didn't leave you. I moved to give Fisher a better life."

And to start over. There'd been too many ghosts back home. Too many memories tied up in places and people. Fisher's mom would always be important to me. I'd always love her, but six years later and I finally was at a place where the grief wasn't thick and cloying, stopping me from moving forward.

"Are you going to show me around or what? Let's FaceTime."

"You're impossible." Reluctantly I agreed and once we were on FaceTime, Eric grinned at me like he'd won the lottery.

"Well, aren't you a sight for sore eyes. Where's the kid?"

"Out exploring the neighborhood on his bike."

Eric furrowed his brow. "He's not helping you out with the work?"

I shrugged. "I don't want him to spend his entire summer painting and mowing and helping me out. He's still a kid. He helps a bit, but I want him to get to know his new neighborhood. Maybe make a friend or two before school starts."

"You're a good dad, and a terrible landscaper. How tall is that grass?"

I turned the camera around and took Eric on a tour of the yard. "You talk as though I'm responsible for it looking like this. But it already looks better. I cleaned up the weeds next to the house first, and gave the patio a quick going-over with the weed whacker and a garden hose." I showed Eric the progress I'd made and then flipped the camera back around.

"It's weird here without you." Eric pouted, but he'd known me my whole life. We met in elementary school and had stuck together ever since. We attended the same college, even if we did major in different things. It had been great to have a friend there. Eric was a constant presence in my life for so long that it *was* weird to know he was so far away now. But the transfer was an opportunity I couldn't pass up.

"It's not like you can't come visit, you know. Now that the movers have been and gone, it's almost livable."

"I'm glad that you kept your standards, Rowan." Eric laughed. Whether it was with me or at me, I couldn't quite decide.

I knew that my decision to move away had come as a shock to him. Thankfully, he'd never tried to talk me out of it. Once I assured him it was what I wanted, what I thought would be best for Fisher, he was on board.

I hated that I couldn't protect Fisher from everything. His experiences at school had ranged from merely okay to miserable, and I doubted he had many great memories associated with his time there. Being the new kid would be tough, but I hoped it would be better than his old school. Stopping kids from bullying my son wasn't something I had control over, but I could control where we lived and getting the hell away from there was the best thing I could do for Fisher. Even though we'd only been here a scant few days, he seemed happier. More relaxed. It was like he too felt the hum of possibility in the air around us.

"I should let you get back to your jungle," Eric said after we'd chatted for another few minutes about nothing in particular. We normally didn't talk on the phone like this, but that was before when he could pop in whenever he wanted. Our friendship had already started to adapt to my new circumstances and I was glad that I wouldn't lose it.

"I'll call you in a couple days when I have the place in some kind of order and I'll take you on the grand tour."

"Sounds good. If you don't get lost in your back yard first." Eric cackled. He always had thought he was the funniest person in the room.

"I'm hanging up now."

Eric blew me a kiss as I ended the call.

There was a time that a gesture like that would have had me second-guessing everything about our friendship. Did he like me? Was he just playing around? What would happen if I kissed him? Eric had been my bisexual awakening, not that he ever knew that. My crush on him had been no more than a flash in the pan. A blip in our friendship that passed as quickly as the fleeting summer of youth.

While my crush on Eric hadn't lasted, my attraction to men had stood the test of time. Between being a closeted teen, then a busy college student, then being married to Fisher's mom, there hadn't been a lot of opportunity for me to date men. And though Fisher's mom had been gone for years now, the idea of dating had always made my skin crawl.

Fisher already got shit from his classmates for being the kid with red hair. The kid with the dead mom. The kid that everyone seemed to want to pick on as a rite of passage or something. Having a dad who dated men definitely wasn't an option.

At least, it didn't used to be. But I could now. In theory at least. In reality, I was too busy embarking on a new life. Too busy doing yard work and unpacking and planning home repairs before I had to officially start at my new position next week to even think about trying to meet someone.

My single status wasn't something I agonized about. At first, I was too heart-sore to worry about being single. And then I was too busy being a single father, working and looking after Fisher. Doing the job of two parents. There simply wasn't room to care about my personal life, or lack thereof.

But Fisher was older now. I'd raised him to be fairly self-sufficient, and while I didn't see myself jumping into the dating pool anytime soon, it felt like it was possible at least. Whoever I ended up with would have to be good with Fisher coming first, though.

With the yard half done, I stopped for a drink and to reapply some sunscreen to my face and neck. Being a redhead myself, I burned to a crisp in no time at all. Spray-on sunscreen was practically a household staple in the summer. After guzzling half a gallon of water straight from the hose, I got back to work. I wanted to at least get the grass cut down to a manageable length then cleaned up so it could be mowed properly.

When I was a kid, old dilapidated buildings and houses had always caught my imagination. The mystery of who lived there and why they'd left had always intrigued me. Sometimes I made up my own theories, but mostly I just wondered if the house ever missed having people in it. They looked lonely, sitting on overgrown lots with darkened windows.

Of course I'd never really grown out of that, or I might not have bought a house that looked lonely in the listing pictures.

I turned the weed whacker off and stowed it in the garden shed. I'd had to run out and buy a lawn mower and the weed whacker, but the previous owners had left a lawn rake and a few other random items. A couple old bike tires, but no bike. An air pump with no hose. Mostly it was junk that would need to be hauled away eventually.

When I exited the shed, I took another look at the lawn and all the fallen grass and decided that I'd had enough for one day. Fisher could rake it up later and I'd run the mower over it tomorrow.

It was nearing dinner time, and while we'd managed to go grocery shopping and stock the cupboards and the fridge, the last thing I wanted to do was cook dinner. I'd spotted a pizza place during our shop, though, and Fisher never said no to pizza.

After dusting the stray grass off my legs, and my arms, and every other part of me, I decided that a quick shower would be in order before I went out into public. It wasn't until I got out of the shower that I realized I'd lost track of time. Fisher had probably returned from his travels as he'd promised not to go too far.

I dressed in a pair of light cotton trousers and a short-sleeved button-up. My poor legs had gotten enough sun for one summer already. Then I went upstairs to get my son.

"Fish, we're going for pizza." I waited at the top of the stairs for his response, but none came.

I checked the bedroom to the right first. Fisher was great for having his headphones on. It was no wonder he hadn't heard me. Only, he wasn't in the bedroom. The same sea of boxes was pushed up against one wall and his bed was against the other. The covers were mussed and there was already laundry on the floor. But no Fisher.

"Fish, come on. Let's get dinner." I poked my head in the other room and found it just as empty as the first.

I didn't panic. It wasn't a big deal that he wasn't back yet. Maybe he was outside. Maybe he made a friend and lost track of time too. I pulled my cell out of my pocket and called his number. Alarm set in when it went to voicemail instead of being answered.

I tried again, and by the time voicemail picked up, my hands were shaking so bad I fumbled my phone. I shouldn't have let him out by himself for so long. Yeah, he was twelve and was more than capable of riding around the block a few times to check out the neighborhood, but he was supposed to have been back by now.

Thundering down the stairs, I checked the rest of the house and the back yard. Coming up empty, I ran for the front door, not bothering with shoes. Who had time for shoes when their kid was missing?

Though I tried to tell myself to stay calm, it didn't work. I was the opposite of cool in a crisis. I could deal with a lot of things, but losing Fisher wasn't one of them. I shot out the front door and called his name. I ran to the end of the driveway and looked up the street for any sign of him and his bright blue bike. Every second that passed when I didn't spot him, another knife drove into my heart.

I looked in the opposite direction, but there was only a quiet, empty street. The sound of lawn mowers droning in the distance. Somewhere nearby, music played. But there wasn't a soul to be seen.

"Fisher!" I shouted, trying to keep the panic at bay. "Fisher!"

CHAPTER 4
GIL

Sunday was my quiet day.

It was my day to sleep in, to drink two cups of coffee, and mindlessly scroll through my phone from the comfort of my bed until an angry stomach forced me into the kitchen. It was my day to eat leftover pizza for breakfast at noon or ice cream if I wanted it. Sundays were a tradition I'd started for myself after Philip and I separated, and even though being single meant every day could be like that, I liked the consistency.

I worked from home, had for years, thanks to the fact my job was computer-based and not people oriented. An extra bonus, considering that, beyond Jack, I didn't care for people. I could log in from my laptop in bed if I wanted to rot, but most of the days were spent in the small back bedroom I'd converted into an office after Philip moved out. The room had the best light, but didn't hold much more than a desk, a chair, and a small bookshelf. Sometimes on Sundays, I tucked myself into the worn-out wingback and read books until dinner time. Sometimes I stared at the wall. It really depended on my mood.

The gusty warmth of the tail end of the summer had me spending most of my free time in the garage, either working on my car or working on my bike. It was nice enough to ride without leathers, but I'd never go without a jacket, and the cool wind that whipped past me when I opened up the throttle was enough to regulate my temperature beneath the tight leather.

That Sunday, I'd gotten up earlier than normal, drank three cups of coffee, got bored of the internet, and decided to take a cruise up to the vista. It would have been a perfect date spot if I cared to date, which I didn't. Unfortunately, that didn't stop all the other people in Sweetwater who did date from coming up and ruining the view. I'd spent more than one night watching the sun go down while a car beside me rocked, the windows opaque with steam.

There had been a time when things like that sounded appealing, sounded fun…but I wasn't that kind of person anymore. It felt childish to say I didn't believe in love, but I had forty-two years of lived experience that proved to me it wasn't a real thing. At least, not in the soul-consuming way I wanted it. It shouldn't have been too much to ask, affection that bordered addiction, obsession. An all-or-nothing kind of thing after years of being given so much less.

None of that mattered.

I stayed alone up on the vista, out of cell phone

range, until the churn of my hungry stomach urged me back onto the bike. Judging by the slow descent of the sun toward the horizon, it was nearly dinner time. I had spent far longer lost to the day up there than I'd planned, and by the time I made it back home, I was beyond irritable. I was hot from the leather, hungry from the lack of food, and annoyed at the loose rattling I'd heard from beneath the frame of the bike as I made it down to the base of the mountain.

It was the end of July and all the families who lived in my neighborhood were gearing up to get back to school. That meant lots of later nights, far more kids roaming the streets than usual, and the occasional ding-dong ditcher. All of it marks of kids trying to enjoy the last scraps of freedom before returning to the routine of school.

If only they could do it a little quieter.

I narrowly avoided running down a group of teenagers who thought it would be fun to shove each other into the street as I made the turn onto my block, and that adrenaline on top of my hunger was enough to have me seeing red by the time I pulled the bike into my driveway. Opening the garage, I cut the engine and rolled her in alongside my project car, flipping down the kickstand and climbing off. She'd need to cool down a bit before I could get in there to see what had come lose, so I stripped off my helmet and jacket, finding both to be heavier and stickier than I remembered. My white undershirt was damp, plastered to my skin, but I was just going to get dirty while I worked on her, so a shower would have to wait.

Instead, I went inside, pouring myself a glass of ice water, which I drank in one go. Immediately, I refilled the glass, then rummaged around the fridge to find something substantial to eat, only to realize going to the store should have been higher on my priority list than fucking off on the top of a mountain. I had orange juice, an onion, two carrots, and a takeout box of Chinese food all haphazardly spread out across the top two shelves of my fridge. The takeout smelled questionable, so I dumped it into the trash, ate both the carrots, then headed back to the garage.

The bike was still a little too hot, so I grabbed a wrench off the top of my box and leaned against the wall to wait. The garage door was still open to let a breeze through, which I didn't intend to be an invitation, but it surely wasn't a deterrent. I watched, flustered, as a gangly-looking red-haired kid with freckles dense as a patch of sand spread over his nose rolled his bicycle along the curb. He looked up when he saw my garage door open, and he angled the front wheel toward my driveway without asking.

"Hey," the kid said, looking tired and dejected. Sweat beaded across his forehead, orange hair sticking every which way but up. "Can you help me?"

"With what?" I asked.

"My bike, the brakes…" he trailed off, frowning.

"Does this look like a bike repair shop?"

"No, but…" The kid tucked his hair behind his ear and fidgeted with his headphones. "My dad won't know how and I…"

I swallowed, setting my water and the wrench down next to my motorcycle.

"And what?" I prompted.

"I need my bike to get to school when it starts and my dad just bought a house and I don't want to ask him for money to take it somewhere."

"Don't kids your age get an allowance?" I asked.

"I did before, but we just moved."

"No chores, then?"

He gave a lopsided shrug. "My dad is doing it all himself for now."

"I'm sure your mom appreciates that," I said.

"My mom's dead."

The kid said it so simply, so matter-of-fact, but his bland delivery wasn't enough to stop the words from piercing through me like a blade.

"I'm sorry, kid."

"I don't really remember her," he said.

"It's still shit."

The corner of his mouth twitched when I cursed, and I tried to imagine what the father of a bright-haired, sour-faced pre-teen would look like. Would he have a similar dusting of freckles, the same unruly kind of hair? Or was this kid a dormant trick of genetics, the only redhead in his family for generations?

"What's your name?" I asked him, only after he'd walked his bike closer to my garage without asking, almost like he'd decided I was going to help him whether I wanted to or not.

"Fisher," he said.

"Fisher what?"

"Fisher Verne."

I snorted. "Didn't your dad tell you not to talk to

strangers? Like, don't they teach stranger danger anymore?"

"I don't know what that is."

"The school system is really failing the new generation," I mumbled, shoving my own hair back from my face. The movement caught Fisher's attention, and his stare flickered to the scar that split the right side of my face.

"How did you get that?" he asked.

"Motorcycle accident when I was younger."

"Did it hurt?"

"Yes," I said.

"Does it still?"

Without thinking, I pressed my fingertips against the bottom edge of the scar, just below my cheekbone.

"Sometimes."

Fisher tilted his head to the side and sized me up in the scrutinizing way that only a teenager can, then having made some silent decision, he walked his bike the rest of the way up the driveway until we were less than three feet apart.

"So, can you help me?" he asked.

I had to give the kid points for his persistence, but his lack of self-awareness was going to get him in trouble one of these days.

"What's wrong with it?"

"The brakes aren't working."

I hummed thoughtfully, gesturing for him to roll it into the shade of the garage alongside my motorcycle. "That sounds like a real problem."

"Yeah," he agreed, more chipper for having gotten his way. "Especially with all the hills here."

"Let's see what you've got, kid. Though it's been awhile since I worked on this kind of bike."

Fisher softly set his hand against the seat of my Triumph, patting it before thinking better and snatching his hand away.

"Do you like motorcycles?" I asked, giving the brakes on his bicycle a squeeze to check the pressure of the calipers.

"My dad hates them," Fisher said, sidestepping around to get closer to mine.

"Your dad sounds smart," I mused, squatting down and confirming one of Fisher's calipers had come loose. "Can you get me the Allen wrench set from the second drawer of that red tool box?"

Fisher's eyes went a little wide, but he went deeper into my garage until he reached my tool box. He opened the drawer and looked down. My knees started to ache from squatting.

"What's an Allen wrench?" he called over his shoulder.

"Are you serious?"

He shot me a death stare.

"The Ikea looking one."

"Oh." Fisher turned back to the box and was quick to grab the bundle of wrenches. "Why didn't you just say so?"

"I did," I muttered, extending my hand to take them from him. He leaned against the wall and folded his arms over his chest, which had me stopping in my tracks. "Nuh-uh. Come over here."

I put the wrenches back into his hand and scooted

over to the side. Fisher grumbled under his breath, but came around to the other side of his bike.

"Earbuds out," I said.

"I don't have any music on."

I blinked at him slowly. "I don't care."

With another stifled argument, he pulled both buds out of his ears and stuffed them into his pocket.

"You want to find the wrench that matches this hole." I pointed to the rusted caliper that hugged his back tire. "See how the whole thing came loose? You have to tighten it back into place and you should be good to go."

It took him three tries to find the right wrench, but once he found it, it look less than a minute for Fisher to get the caliper back into place.

"That was easy," he said, trying to pass me back the wrench set.

I shook my head, rising to my feet. "You can put them back. You know where they go."

The excitement from completing his bike repair was fleeting as it came with more work, and I called out to stop him at the back of the garage, "Get that oil can off the top while you're there. You might as well give the lines a quick grease."

I talked Fisher through how to grease the brake line and check the connection in case anything came loose on him again. He didn't need to be told to take the can back to the tool box when we were done with it, and I smiled to myself at what a quick learner he was.

"There," I said, tossing him a dirty shop rag for his hands. "You're good to go."

"Fisher!"

A terrified and desperate-sounding cry echoed from

the end of the block, and instead of looking concerned, Fisher looked bored.

"Fisher!"

His name again, and Fisher pulled his earbuds out of his pocket and popped them back into place.

I looked past him, toward the sound of his name, when my stare landed on the man who must be his father. The genetics did not skip a generation because the man I saw power-walking down my block had the same bright red hair, the same dusting of freckles over his cheekbones, except he was taller and more muscular, but still on the small side.

"He's here," I called out with a raise of my hand to get his attention since Fisher clearly wasn't going to make himself known.

Fisher kicked his kickstand and wheeled his bike out of my garage and down the driveway toward the man I assumed to be his father. The older redhead raced up my driveway, grabbing Fisher by both arms and giving him a shake before hauling him into a hug. His relief turned to concern, and then to anger when he saw me in the garage, arms folded in front of my chest.

He and I were opposites, me in my torn black jeans, black leather boots, and dirty white t-shirt. Him with his loose cotton chinos and tucked in, plaid short-sleeved button-up.

"Fisher," the man said, eyes narrowed at me, even as they took stock of me from my boots up to my hair. "Are you okay? What are you doing here? I expected you home hours ago."

"My phone died," Fisher explained with a careless shrug. "And my bike broke. This guy helped me."

"This guy." He frowned. "That's rude, Fisher. What's his name?"

Fisher glanced at me over his shoulder. He'd never asked.

"Gil," I said, before either of them could. "Gil Valentine."

"Fisher," he said to his son. "You can't just…"

"He's fine," I interrupted, waving off the man's concerns. "Just had a loose caliper on his bike and he didn't want to bother you with it. He saw me out here working on my bike and I offered to help."

Fisher rolled his eyes, both of us knowing that was a half-truth at best.

"Well, thank you," the man said, still protectively patting his hands all over his son as if to check him for injuries. "We just moved to town, and…"

Apparently the man had as much of a problem stringing sentences together as his son did. The only thing he had going for him was he was very nice to look at.

"No harm, no foul," I assured him.

My motorcycle was definitely ready to work on and seemed far more interesting than the lack of conversation the kid's dad was trying to have with me, so I turned around and bent over to pick up the wrench I'd discarded on Fisher's arrival.

The man choked a bit, clearing his throat when I looked over my shoulder at him.

"I'm Rowan, by the way. I should thank you properly for helping my son."

"No thanks necessary, Rowan." I waved him off and turned back to my bike because looking at him brought up too many dormant feelings that I'd long since forgotten. Feelings like interest, like curiosity, like arousal.

"I insist," Rowan protested, but I wasn't having it.

"Have a good night, Rowan and Fisher Verne." Then I grabbed the garage door remote off my bike and closed the door on them both.

CHAPTER 5
ROWAN

"I'm sorry, Dad." Fisher dragged his feet up the steps and into the house after putting his bike away. My heart had calmed down the moment I laid eyes on him, unharmed, in the garage we'd spotted the day we moved in—the one with the classic car.

Now my heart raced for an entirely different reason.

Gil Valentine was the hottest man I'd ever laid eyes on. He wasn't gym buff, but the man had muscles. Even more than his fantastic ass, it was his eyes that drew me in. Ice green and cold, their light color a contrast against his dark hair. Dark except for the shock of white at the end of a scar that cut the left side of his face from forehead to cheekbone.

And the *scar*.

That was hot.

It didn't take away from his appeal; instead it added to it.

I followed Fisher into the kitchen and watched as he poured himself a glass of juice. It struck me out of the blue sometimes just how much older Fisher was now. He could pour his own juice. Make his own meals. Ride his bike around the neighborhood by himself. Sometimes it was hard to loosen my hold on him, but he couldn't stay small forever.

"There's a small chance that I might have panicked prematurely, just make sure you check in more often next time. Send a text once in a while as proof of life, okay."

Fisher rolled his eyes as he chugged his juice. "What's for dinner?" he asked when his glass was empty. "Can we get Chinese? I rode by this one place today. Ooh, or we could get burgers."

"I could whip something up really quick."

Fisher put on his best kiss-ass expression. The wide eyes, the angelic smile. "But you've worked so hard today. You deserve a break."

"So you can cook."

"After a hard day's work, do you really want to eat the food a twelve year-old would make? Toaster waffles aren't substantial enough to compensate for all the energy you burned."

I raised my eyebrow and Fisher's face fell.

"Did I lay it on too thick?"

"A bit, yes. We'll do burgers. Did you want to come with me to pick them up or stay here and jump in the shower while I'm gone?"

Fisher was an adolescent boy that had been in the sun all day. His adventures had left him a little ripe. "You should wash that sunscreen off."

Fisher narrowed his eyes. I always thought it made him resemble me the most when he did that. It was almost like looking at a picture of my younger self.

"Are you saying I stink?"

"I would never say something so hurtful." I grinned at him. "Do you want fries or onion rings?"

He paused to think, his brow furrowing. "You get fries. I'll get onion rings and we can share and compare."

From the time he was able to eat grown-up food, Fisher had been obsessed with onion rings. He was very particular about them. The batter had to be just right. Not too thick and it had to stick to the onion. Batter that flaked off with the first bite never failed to disappoint him.

I grabbed my keys off the counter and stuffed them in my pocket. "You shower. I'll get food and I'll be back soon. If you unpack the DVD player, we can watch a movie."

Fisher rolled his eyes at me again. It had become his favorite response to most things I said lately. "We can just stream something from my phone right to the TV."

"You forget that I was born in the late 1900s, Fisher. Some of this new technology escapes me."

"Don't blame me because you're stuck in the dark ages." He laughed as he headed for the bathroom. "Don't forget extra pickles for my burger."

"I'll be back soon."

Once I was outside, I had to force myself not to make the short trip to Gil's house. He'd clearly had enough human interaction for one day, at least that was the impression I got when he shut the door to his garage.

I backed out of the driveway and rolled the window down to enjoy the late summer air. It was best at night, once the heat of the day had gone and the sun was lower in the sky. The scent of barbeque drifted on the air as I turned the music up and sang along in my more than slightly off key way until I reached the restaurant.

Beefy's was on the list of top ten best burger joints in the city. Before I moved here, I'd done my research. I knew where to get the best food, what pharmacy was closest to my house, and where the nearest fire station, police station, and hospital were. I also knew what pizza place the locals loved best. These were all important things to know.

The restaurant had a cozy vibe, with a couple big couches in the front where people could sit and wait for their to-go orders. The main restaurant was deceptively large inside, with a patio around back for more seating. One day I'd have to bring Fisher here to eat.

A girl, wearing a nametag reading Beth, with blue hair all done up in a messy bun on the top of her head greeted me at the counter with a smile. "Welcome to Beefy's What can I get for you?"

"What's good here?"

Beth shot me a smile. "Everything's good. But I recommend the Jack burger. It's got all the fixings, plus Monterey Jack cheese on a sesame seed bun. That or the bacon mushroom burger. All our burgers come with fries, onion rings, or salad."

"Could I get two Jack burgers, one with extra pickles and onion rings. One with fries." On a whim, I thought about Gil Valentine, the hunk who fixed my son's bike and asked for nothing in return. It wasn't every day that strangers went out of their way to be nice to other people. "Could I also get... a bacon cheeseburger with fries?"

"Sure thing. Was there anything else?" Beth punched my order into the machine.

"That's everything. Thank you."

"Your total is $54.40. Will that be cash or card?"

Opening my wallet, I peeled out three twenty dollar bills and handed them over. "Keep the change."

"Thank you!" Beth's already friendly smile grew brighter. "It'll be about fifteen minutes. If you leave your number, we can text you when it's ready for pick up."

"That would be great, actually." I hadn't had much of a chance to explore my new town. I'd been too busy unpacking, or taming the yard, or taking care of the other ten million tasks that I had to do before I started back to work soon. There just hadn't been time to wander and look around. Fifteen minutes wasn't a lot, but it was something.

Leaving my number with Beth, I ventured out onto the sidewalk. Picking a direction, I decided to take a right. I passed an honest-to-God shoe store a few doors down. I didn't know those still existed. I thought by now that the department stores had swallowed the shoe stores whole. It was a pleasant surprise. Further down was a health food store and one dedicated to tabletop games.

The jewel of the block turned out to be a little craft brewery called Top Hops. The inside was decorated in mostly blond wood tones, and with the lights on, it gave the building a warm glow, sort of like how I felt after three drinks. On another whim, I bought a six-pack of bottles. The beer promised to be tropical, majestic, and robust.

I could tell myself that I was just missing Eric and my other friends back home. I could tell myself that I was just trying to be friendly. Neighborly. The truth was that I was no better than a kid with a crush. Gil Valentine was the most attractive man I'd ever seen. And he'd been nice to Fisher. Of course I didn't expect an adult to be awful to a kid, but it had happened before.

It wasn't until after I collected the food and got back in my car that it occurred to me that I might be about to make a fool of myself. Gil had shut the garage door in my face. If he'd been able to slam it, he might have done so. Clearly, he didn't want to be bothered. But I was committed to thanking him properly. At home, I parked in the driveway and dug the container with Gil's order in it out of the bag. After I collected it, and the beer, I kicked my door shut with my foot and headed for Gil's front door.

A deep breath didn't help calm me down at all. Nor did the three others I took while I waited for Gil to answer his door. I was about to ring the bell again when the door swung open and Gil appeared, freshly showered. His hair dripped onto the collar of his shirt.

Pushing the fact that he'd been naked not two minutes ago to the back of my mind, I held out the burger and the six-pack. And said… nothing. My mouth and my brain weren't currently cooperating.

Gil arched an eyebrow.

"What's this?" His gaze flicked to the items, then back to mine.

"Food. Dinner." I cleared my throat. "I got you dinner. And drinks. For your help. With Fisher."

I wanted to die. There wasn't a hole deep enough for me to bury my shame. Since when was I incapable of putting together a full, coherent sentence?

"I told you that no thanks were necessary." Gil didn't reach for the beer or the burger, but I didn't relent.

"And I wanted to do something nice for someone who went out of his way to help my son. Please, it's not much. It's just a burger and some beer."

Gil's jaw ticked. "You don't give up easy, do you?"

"It's the single dad in me. If I give up, there's no one to pick up the slack." As true as it was, it still shocked me that I'd said it at all. Clearly, I couldn't win for losing today. I was either all but incoherent, or I was over-sharing.

Gil's shoulders dropped and the tension bled out of him. Not entirely, but at least enough where I no longer felt like I was unwelcome.

"Is that from Beefy's?" Gil looked at the nondescript cardboard takeout container.

"It is." I thrust the burger toward him. My stomach gave a happy kick when he took it from my grasp. Feeling hopeful, I tried to hand him the six-pack.

Gil's lip curled. "You went to Top Hops too, I see. You should sample that one for yourself."

"But I got it for you."

"Tell you what, you keep that one. Think of it as a welcome to the neighborhood gift." I didn't know Gil at all, but I had the feeling he was up to something.

"It's that bad, is it?"

If I thought Gil was hot before, nothing compared to how gorgeous he was when he smiled. He reached for the beer and took one of the bottles out. Using his teeth, he cracked it open, then handed it to me. The dare was silent, but it was there.

I raised the bottle to my lips trying not to think of the

fact that it had just been in Gil's mouth. I took a sip… and then turned and spit it out into the bushes that edged the stairs.

"That was terrible." My body shuddered. "Oh, God. That was… what's in that?"

Gil shrugged, his smile still clinging to his expression. "I don't know. Horse piss probably."

"Sorry I tried to poison you."

"No harm done."

"I'm going to go home and dump these down the drain. Enjoy your dinner, Gil. And thanks again for helping Fisher today. See you around."

Maybe.

If I didn't die of embarrassment.

First the stuttering babble. Then the TMI. Then the disgusting beer.

I was on a roll.

CHAPTER 6
GIL

The burger was good, but the adorable flush that colored Rowan's face when he struggled his way through a sentence was better. He'd stumbled backward down my front steps, raising his hand in a sort of awkward and embarrassed save before spinning on his heel and racing down the street.

I figured he and his son must have moved into the old McAllister house at the end of the block. The house had sat empty since old man McAllister died earlier in the year because no one had been brave enough to make the purchase, considering all the work the place was going to need. Besides how overgrown the yard had become, there was no way Rowan was going to get away without getting a new roof before winter and new gutters before spring.

Licking bacon grease off my fingers, I found myself wondering what sort of situation would drive a man with an almost-teenager to move into such a rundown place, but we all had our burdens. Rowan Verne, with his pressed pants and button-up shirts, didn't seem like the type to have any real problems besides the state of his house and his grasp of the English language, but I knew as well as anyone that looks could be deceiving.

I was halfway finished with the burger when I heard another knock at my door. I'd already had more visitors today than I liked to have, but the last thing I expected was to find Rowan Verne on my porch for a second time that night. He had a fresh six-pack in his hand, this one a generic stout from the liquor store down the road. I opened the door and leaned against the frame, unable to stop myself from smirking down at him.

He was so much smaller than me, so delicate, so proper with his blush and the nervous way he shifted his weight from foot to foot.

So flustered.

So fucking *pretty*.

"Rowan," I greeted him, reaching up to scratch an itch on my right cheek.

His eyes tracked the movement, pupils dilating when my hand fell away. His stare fell at the same time, lingering on my mouth before I cleared my throat and brought him back to the present. His cheeks darkened, making the constellation of freckles across the bridge of his nose appear a deeper shade of brown than they had earlier.

"That beer was horrid," he said, smiling in a way that looked almost painful. "So, consider this a replacement."

"You really didn't need to do that."

"I wanted to."

He thrust the six-pack against my chest, and I reacted

quickly, coming up with both hands to grab the bottles before they fell. I caught his hand in the process, his wrist, the fine bones of his arm twisting beneath my grasp like he wanted to move, but didn't dare. His skin was cool to the touch, soft.

There were more freckles.

God, I bet he had freckles everywhere.

Pushing the thought of Rowan's potentially freckled ass and thighs out of my mind, I took a step backward, carton of beer clutched in my greasy hand.

"Well, thank you." I lifted the beer and gave him a quick smile. "Did you want to come in and have a drink?"

Rowan looked over his shoulder and gave me a half-shrug.

"I can't. I mean, it's not a good idea. It's just that Fisher's at home, so…" He trailed off.

"Enough said."

A deafening silence slid down between us, and Rowan looked like he wanted to jackhammer a hole into my porch so he could crawl into the earth and never emerge. He was so awkward, I had to put him out of his misery.

"Thanks again, Rowan."

I closed the door part of the way, still able to watch him again stumble backward off my porch toward his car. He caught himself before falling on his ass, but the save was far from graceful. I kept the door halfway closed, something prickling at the back of my neck while I watched him fumble keys into the ignition and get the car into gear. He backed out of my driveway with another wave, and then everything was the kind of quiet I'd long been used to.

I closed the door the rest of the way and bolted the locks, taking the beer into the kitchen and dropping it onto the counter beside my burger. Suddenly, I was no longer hungry. At least, not for food.

I'd gone two years without sex.

Two years without wanting it and very nearly two years without thinking about it.

How had a little red-haired stranger—a single dad, no less—shown up on my porch out of nowhere and kick started a libido I sincerely thought Philip had packed up with his own things when he left me?

Jack was going to have a field day when he found out.

Wait.

What?

No.

Jack wasn't going to find out. It wasn't as if I was going to fuck Rowan, let alone date him. There was no reason for my best friend to even know my new neighbor's name, let alone the fact the way he blushed sent blood rushing between my legs. Hell, Jack would probably think I got body-snatched if I started showing an interest in sex again. He'd put the lucky person onto a pedestal and worship them until his dying breath for bringing his precious best friend back from the dead.

But…

I hadn't been dead. Grieving, maybe. Readjusting, sure.

I wasn't unhappy with the course my life had taken since separating from Philip, but I knew myself better than I ever had, and I knew a man like Rowan was not a match for me. He had a kid for one, and I was not a kid person. It didn't matter that I'd helped Fisher with his bike. I'd just been waiting for mine to cool down so there hadn't been anything better to do. It was a courtesy, not a change of heart.

And Rowan?

As nice as he was to look at, there was no way we'd be compatible in bed. He turned the color of strawberries after bringing me a beer; what would happen to him when I got my mouth right up against his ear and wanted to talk him through it? How hot would his skin burn with my fingers against it?

No.

Stop.

Another knock on the door. I knew without looking it was Rowan.

I knew he was back, either with or without his son, with a change of heart and a desire to share a drink with me after all.

I knew I couldn't let him in.

I popped the top off one of the bottles and went back to the front door, making sure my dick was in line before undoing the deadbolt and opening up for a third time that night.

"Rowan," I greeted him again.

He was still red, still stammering, still looking like something I wanted to take apart with my teeth.

"Fisher was…I got home…he was playing video games."

Rowan paused like I was meant to commiserate with him over that, but I had no idea why.

"Okay," I drawled, raising the bottle to my mouth and taking a long pull.

It was a good beer.

"So, if you wanted to still have a drink…" He pulled his lips between his teeth, stare locked on my mouth. His nostrils flared when he exhaled.

"You were probably right about it not being a good idea," I said.

Rowan was an open book, his expression falling as soon as the words left my mouth. His dejected frown had me feeling beyond cruel, but there wasn't any good to come from sharing a drink with a man like Rowan Verne.

"Oh."

"Oh," I repeated.

"Uhm." Rowan tilted his head to the side, brow furrowed. "Why not?"

"Why not what?"

"Why isn't it a good idea?" he asked.

"Your son's at home," I offered, even though it was a flimsy reason.

"He's fine." Rowan's voice cracked. "He's practically a teenager and he's wrapped up in his game."

"It's just…not, Rowan."

He swallowed and angled his chin up, trying to make himself taller than he was, which was honestly a shame because I liked him short. Liked the idea of him beneath me in more ways than one.

"Do you…"

The unanswered question hung between us.

"Do I what?" I prompted.

The beer was slippery and cold in my hand, so I set it

down on the side table near the door so I didn't drop it. I wiped the wetness off on the front of my thigh, and Rowan's stare tracked my hand down there as well.

"Do you…are you seeing someone? Did I read you wrong?"

I huffed, shaking my head and looking down at my feet. My hair fell into my face, the shock of white giving Rowan a halo effect if I peered up through my lashes.

"I'm not seeing anyone," I said.

"I'm not either. I mean, Fisher's mom, she…"

I raised my hand to stop him. "We don't need to do all that."

"Right. Sorry. I haven't…"

Another sentence lost to the abyss of his mind.

"I'm not looking to make friends, Rowan," I warned, taking a step to the side to expose more of the doorway. "If you come in, it's for one thing and one thing only."

"And that thing's not a beer."

"You can have one, but…no. It's not for a beer."

Rowan gave a quick and jerky nod, blinking up at me like he'd just had a conversation and made a decision I wasn't quite privy to.

"That's fine," he said, stepping off the porch and into my house.

I moved to make more room for him, then pushed the door closed behind him. My arm stretched above his head, and he walked backward, pressing his back against the door, all while staring up at me with blue eyes so blown they were almost entirely black. He was so close I could hear the way his exhales trembled. I could see his pulse battering against the side of his neck. I leaned down and kissed him there, sucking him into my mouth like I could somehow steady his heartbeat by kissing him hard enough.

"Oh, God." He was already breathless, his hands came up to my waist and grabbed me for balance.

I kissed my way around to the front of his throat, up the underside of his jaw, his chin, and finally his mouth. Rowan tasted like that shitty beer from Top Hops and stolen french fries from the takeout bag. He parted his lips for me instantly, kissing me back with far more skill and talent than I'd expected from him.

"Bedroom," I muttered against his mouth, reaching down and grabbing him by the backs of his thighs. He got the message quickly, wrapping both legs around my waist and his arms around my neck.

I didn't need to see where I was going; I knew my house like the back of my hand, and I kissed Rowan out of the living room and down the hallway, straight into my bedroom and onto my bed.

"Take your clothes off, Row. Show me what we're working with here."

Rowan hummed, tearing open his brown leather belt. "Not much."

"I'll be the judge of that."

I reached back and rucked up my shirt, pulling it up and over my head before dropping it on the floor. I made quick work of my pants, my underwear, stare focused at the naked man on my bed and the thick, hard cock between his legs.

He had freckles *everywhere*.

Rowan tugged his cock with one hand, covering his face with the other, scooting up the bed until his head was nestled in my pillows.

"You're gorgeous," I assured him, taking lube from the nightstand.

He slid his hand down to cover his mouth, giving me a slow and appreciative onceover. "So are you."

"I want to fuck you so badly, Rowan, but I don't have any condoms."

"That's fine. I…it's been awhile and it's fine."

"Are you sure?" I asked.

He stroked his shaft, a pearl of precum beading against the perfect slit of his dick.

"It's fine," he said again.

I climbed onto the bed and dropped the lube by his feet, taking his knees into my hands and spreading his legs wide. Not only did he have freckles everywhere, but he flushed pink everywhere too. He looked like a dessert, and I was going to eat him until I'd had my fill.

"Can I rim you?" I dragged my hand down the inside of his thigh, teasing my fingertips over his pucker. His skin was soft, burning hot.

"You don't have to, I'm not…not prepared really."

"Can I rim you?" I asked again, my own cock aching to be buried inside of his hot hole, coated in lube and spit.

"Yes." He covered his face again, and I didn't know what he was so embarrassed about, but I had his consent and that was more than enough for me.

Rowan smelled like peppermint soap and sweat, and when I sealed my lips around his hole and sucked, the sound that left his throat had my dick leaking into my sheets. Digging my fingers into his thighs, I spread his legs apart, licking and fucking his asshole until there was a wet spot on his stomach and a puddle beneath him on the sheets. He thrashed around, moaning and jerking his cock while I sloppily used my mouth to get him ready, and when I added a lube-slick finger to the mix, he grabbed my hair and pulled up *hard*.

"I'll come," he warned.

"That's the point," I reminded him, deciding to ease off him a little so he didn't finish before I even got started.

One finger and then two, then three. The sheets were so far gone by the time I covered my cock with lube and pushed into him, but I didn't care. The only thing that mattered was the impossibly tight grip of his body as I fed my erection into his ass, inch by inch, and the way his chin quivered silently when I seated myself fully inside of him.

"Look at you," I whispered, brushing his sweat-damp hair back off his forehead. "Look how good you take my cock up your ass."

"Your mouth," he muttered, one hand still in my hair, the other half covering his face again.

I swatted it away, needing to see every micro-expression he made, especially the ones leading up to the orgasm I was about to fuck right out of him.

"What about my mouth?"

"It's filthy."

I hummed, dragging my nose across his cheek and hovering less than an inch away from his mouth. "It tastes like you."

I kissed him again, starting to fuck him with short and slow thrusts so we could both get used to the feel of each other's bodies. Rowan was so flustered still, so tense, forgetting to kiss me back for how lost he was in the rest of what we were doing.

"Come on, Rowan," I coaxed, adjusting my hips to find the angle that would drive him mad. "Open up and let me get in there. There you go. Oh, fuck. I wish you could see yourself. Wish you could feel how tight and slippery your ass is."

I pulled back, breaking the kiss so I could look down to the place our bodies were joined. He was a wet mess, spit and lube streaked across his balls and his thighs. I traced the mixture around his pink and stretched rim, groaning when he shivered and clenched down on my shaft.

"I fucked so much spit into your ass with my tongue, Row. You're so fucking sloppy and wet for me. It's the hottest thing I've ever seen."

It wasn't a lie.

Rowan, spread out beneath me with my dick disappearing up his ass was one for the books. I'd jerk off thinking about it for the rest of my life, even if I never saw him naked again after tonight.

"Jesus, Gil."

"Is it too much?" I asked, kissing the corner of his mouth. "Did you want to stop?"

I didn't want to be too much, but I didn't want to stop either. For some reason, I needed him to know exactly what he did to me.

"No one has said things like that to me before."

"Have they *done* things like that to you?" I asked, nipping at his jaw.

"No," he rasped.

I went still, wanting him, but not wanting to push

him beyond what he would enjoy. "I can stop if you don't like it."

"I don't want you to stop any of it," he whispered. "I want to come."

"I can make you come, darling. Don't you worry about that."

The endearment left my mouth before I could stop it, a long-forgotten sentiment that had no place in a bed meant purely for fucking. I didn't bother trying to take it back, and Rowan didn't ask me to. Instead, I shifted my weight to balance over him, thrusting long, hard, and deep into his spit- and lube-slicked body.

"Gil. Oh, fuck. Gil. Gil." He recited my name over and over, sometimes sounding like a prayer and sometimes like a plea.

"You take it like you were made for it," I murmured, covering his hand with my own and bringing it between our bodies. I curled his fingers around his cock and mine around his fist. "Show me how you like to come, Rowan."

He screwed his eyes closed, looking like he was in pain, but the long and tight pulls up the length of his cock led me to believe it was anything *but* pain. It was hard to keep pace fucking him when all I wanted to do was watch him get himself off all over our hands, but every time my tip dragged across his prostate, his muscles tensed and squeezed, pulling me closer to my own end.

"I'm close," he whimpered.

"Good." I licked his jaw and sank my teeth into his earlobe. "Come on my hand, Rowan. That's it. There you go. Oh, fuck."

His entire body tensed, and then Rowan's eyes flew open.

Two seconds later, hot cum spurted across my fingers. I crashed our mouths back together, hips snapping once, twice more. I wanted more than anything to come inside of him, but he was too blissed out to have that conversation and I was barely hanging on to the last threads of sanity.

"Look how hard you make me come, Rowan. You're making me fucking come." I said, words tumbling out of my mouth as I pulled out of him at the very last moment. Our hands were still wrapped around his cock and I shot my load across his cum-slick dick, our tangled fingers, the smattering of freckles on his stomach. Rowan shivered as he watched me spill onto his skin, another burst of cum leaking from his dick before he tore both of our hands away from his shaft with a strangled cry.

I milked out the end of my release, then collapsed beside him on the bed, chest heaving. Closing my eyes, I puffed a breath out of my mouth in an attempt to dislodge the sweaty hair from my forehead, but it was no use. Those strands weren't going anywhere, and neither was I. My legs no longer worked, and it was none other than awkwardly unassuming Rowan Verne who'd given me one of the fiercest orgasms of my entire life.

"Jesus," he said after some time had passed. I turned to the side and watched him wipe our cum off his fingers and onto my sheets, which should have offended me but honestly…I was too tired to care. I'd had my face halfway up his ass before we'd gotten down to business, but he couldn't be bothered to use his tongue to taste the mess we'd left behind?

It was just one more reason that Rowan was no good for me, or more likely, I was no good for him. Forcing myself to school my expression, I sat on the edge of the bed, giving him my back while I regained my composure and my breath.

"So," he said from behind me, still breathless himself. "What about that beer?"

CHAPTER 7
ROWAN

When Gil was fucking me, it was like being in the eye of a hurricane. Everything around me could have been tearing apart, but there was only him and me in the center of everything.

Gil had… changed me? Was that too dramatic?

Probably. I was half giddy, half terrified of what we'd done. Of what it meant.

To him. To me. In general.

The truth was I had relatively little experience with men. Or women. I'd always been kind of awkward. Besides my short-lived crush on Eric and meeting my wife in college, there'd been a couple nervous encounters with other girls as a horny teen, but not much else. I had a feeling that even if I'd been with half the football team *and* the cheer squad, nothing would have compared to the way Gil fucked me. I never knew it could be like that.

With his back to me, I suddenly felt shy and far more exposed than when all his attention was on me. I wasn't good at people. I wasn't good at knowing what they wanted or making friends. In general, being a single dad had taught me to care a little less about what people thought of me. All that mattered was making sure Fisher was looked after.

But Fisher needed some independence from me, and I needed to have my own life again. I'd wanted to make friends with Gil. He was gorgeous, and cool for lack of a better word. He was the embodiment of every guy I'd ever dreamed of having. All long legs and sexy arms and that scar on his face? I wanted to kiss it.

Was that weird? That was probably weird.

Searching desperately for something to say, I defaulted back to the reason I came back over and asked about that beer.

Gil's tone of voice was gruff, but not in the sexy way like it was before. He was more distant. Like he just realized he made a mistake.

"Sure," he said, "a beer."

But he didn't sound sure. Maybe I should go, I thought. I sat up too fast and hissed when the rigorous sex we had made itself known to my body. I wasn't injured, just far more tender than I thought I'd be.

"Holy crap."

"You okay?" Gil turned so he was kind of looking at me. Like the only reason he had to look at me was because it was his obligation to check on me after rearranging my guts.

I winced again as I slid out of bed and stood clumsily in Gil's room. "I'm fine. I just didn't think it would hurt this much after."

The atmosphere in the room changed and he turned

to face me fully. The set of his jaw indicated that he was displeased.

"Rowan, were you a virgin?"

I snorted. "Gil, I have a kid. You've met him. About five-foot-five, red hair."

Gil's expression darkened. "You know what I mean."

"Well, no. But like… also maybe? I'm not sure what you count as virgin. If you're asking if I've ever had anything in my ass, the answer is yes. If you're asking if I've had a man's cock up my ass before, the answer is no."

"You should've told me." Gil's hands clenched and unclenched at his sides.

"Why?" Suddenly sick of the direction of this conversation, I hunted for my pants. I was covered in cum and didn't really want to go home smelling like sex, but maybe I could sneak in and make a beeline for the shower. Or maybe I could drive around until after Fisher was supposed to be in bed and then sneak in.

"Because you should have."

"Yeah, well, you should have told me that it mattered to you."

I didn't know where this sudden burst of backbone came from. It had been a long day. A long month, really. Locating my pants, I tried to put them on, but anger swelled up in me like a storm surge. Grabbing onto the waist of my pants, I tried to shove my foot in and failed. And when I finally succeeded in getting both feet in, I realized my pants were backwards.

"Fucking, fucking, fuck." I cursed as I tried to step out of my pants. I wobbled and nearly fell over, but a strong hand caught my arm. I looked up at Gil, whose thunderous expression had eased off.

"Rowan, stop. It's fine."

I narrowed my gaze. "Is it? It didn't seem fine a minute ago."

"It's fine." Gil repeated, then helped me out of my pants. "Did you want a shower? You're covered in cum."

He stated it like it was no big deal. *Water is wet. Fire is hot. Rowan is covered in cum.*

"That would be great, actually."

Gil released my arm and motioned toward the en suite. "It's all yours."

I looked Gil in the eyes and waited for some kind of indication of how he was feeling. What he was thinking. Was he mad at me? It felt like I was being dismissed and I tried not to take it personally, but I couldn't help feeling a little rejected.

"Thanks." I padded off to the bathroom and shut myself inside. Gil's bathroom suited him. It seemed like such a dumb thing to say, but it was all dark walls and white subway tiles. Gil was the only person I'd ever met who had plants in his bathroom. They added a touch of life to the room that it would have sorely missed without them.

I wanted to decorate my bathroom at home just like this. But maybe with one of those fancy rain shower-heads or a deep clawfoot tub with the sloped back. The kind that you could fill up to your chin with water and soak your life away in.

Despite my urge to use all the hot water, I kept my shower short. A weird kind of thrill shot through me when I used Gil's products to give myself a quick clean. Now I was going to smell like him regardless.

Long before I was ready, I turned the water off, dried myself, and slid back into my clothes. I frowned at the sight of Gil's empty bed. There wasn't going to be a shred of evidence that I'd even been here. Nothing but a rapidly drying wet spot and some cum on the edge of the sheets where I'd wiped it off my fingers, too scared to taste it. Too overwhelmed to do it in case I'd have to analyze what it meant later. But I'd set a trap for myself, because I was still thinking about it and the more I thought about it, the more it felt like a missed opportunity.

A shooting star I'd forgotten to wish on.

I found Gil in the kitchen. His back was to me when I came in and I had half a second to appreciate the wide expanse of his bare shoulders, the taper of his waist, and the way his jeans sat low on his hips. Then Gil turned around. His torn jeans and sockless feet made my mouth go dry. He hadn't even zipped his pants. The fly hung open revealing the nothing he was wearing underneath them.

It would take almost no convincing to get me on my knees in front of him. I'd never sucked a dick before but, God, did I want to suck his.

Gil crossed the room, his bare feet almost silent as he went to the fridge, then approached me with a bottle of beer.

"Thanks." I said, unsure where to look. Gil was like the sun, too bright to look directly at, but he must have taken it as an insult.

"There a problem?" He stepped back and leaned against his counter. He was the kind of guy who just exuded confidence. He crossed one foot over the other and let the counter take his weight as he sipped at his beer.

"No, just, uh… can you zip your pants up?" Maybe if I smashed the bottle of beer over my head hard enough, I'd lose consciousness and be put out of my misery.

"You've seen me naked, Rowan. I've been inside of you."

My dick twitched when he said my name. It was dumb. How was I suddenly seventeen and useless around hot men again?

"Yeah, that's the problem." I cleared my throat then took a sip of beer. "You're kind of distracting."

"Only kind of? Looks like I need to up my game." Gil held my gaze while he reached down, beer in one hand, and dragged his zipper up slowly with the other. I felt the rasp of the metal teeth biting into my soul.

Suddenly out of things to say, I took a long slow sip of the beer. It was better than the donkey piss I'd first brought over, but there was still room for improvement.

"I love your bathroom," I blurted, for lack of anything better to talk about. "It suits you."

I thought of how nice it might have been to have shared that space with Gil. To have seen him stripped bare, vulnerable. To lick the water off his—*stop it*—I told myself. There would be no water licking and no shower sharing. There would be friendly beers now and then because that's what neighbors did. "I have to pretty much redo every room in the house. Eventually. Some rooms are more important than others, so who know when I'll get around to my bathroom. But yours is nice."

"You bought the old McAllister place up the street, right?"

"Yeah. The yard is still in a bit of a state, but it's getting there. It's a lot of work for one person, but I at least want the yard done before I start work."

"Yeah, once their old man passed away, his kids cleaned the place out, slapped a for sale sign in the yard, and never looked back. You've got your work cut out for you."

Gil smirked and something inside me twisted up in a knot. His words felt like a challenge. Or maybe I was too raw after what we'd done. Too upside-down about all the things I felt for Gil. My attraction had seemed so one-sided at first, and then everything between us happened so fast, I was still trying to catch up.

"I've got it covered." I frowned at my beer and picked at the label.

"Never said you didn't."

I felt the hairs at the back of my neck stand up. My throat tightened and I tried not to look at Gil's bare chest, or the bits of skin I could see through his holey jeans, or his fucking feet. Feet had no business being attractive, but Gil's appeal clearly went from head to toe in a literal sense for me.

"If I did something to offend you, or if I wasn't good or something, I'm sorry."

"Wasn't good?" Gil seemed almost affronted by that. "What do you mean if you weren't good, you're sorry?"

"It's not like I knew what I was doing, and I know this was like a one-time thing, but I don't want it to be awkward between us, and I feel like you're mad at me."

For the longest time Gil didn't speak. When he did, his voice had lost that hard edge to it. But it was almost worse now, because the gruffness was better than the barely hidden sadness in Gil's words.

"You were far from bad, Rowan. Trust me on that."

The heat that flooded my face could rival the surface of the sun.

I made myself look Gil in the eyes. He looked more relaxed, like there'd been some kind of storm going on inside him as well, but now there was nothing but calm in his eyes.

"I should get home and check on my son." I could have texted Fisher if I was that concerned, but I'd long ago mastered the art of using my child to get out of situations. I might have moved, but my habits had moved with me.

"Thanks for the beer. But, Rowan, let me buy the next ones."

I couldn't help but smile at that. "Are you sure? Third time might be the charm. At least this batch was drinkable. The guy who sold me the first six had a bit of a shit-eating grin when I went back for something else."

I finished my beer and handed the empty to Gil. I didn't hope that Gil's fingers would brush against mine as he took the bottle, giving me one last touch. Which was good because it didn't happen. I pulled my hand away and tucked it in my pocket. "Yeah, uh, thanks for... just... thanks. I'll see you around, I guess."

"See you around, Rowan."

Gil stayed in the kitchen while I walked myself to the front door and stuffed my feet in my shoes. I walked out of Gil's house wondering if things would ever start to feel normal again.

CHAPTER 8
GIL

Three days later and I hadn't been able to stop thinking about Rowan Verne and the bumbling way he tricked me into taking his virginity. I also couldn't stop thinking about the way his whole body quivered when he had an orgasm, and I definitely couldn't stop thinking about how hard he made *me* come. Unfortunately, with all of that, I was forced to remember the way I treated him afterward.

It wasn't my fault.

The whole thing had caught me off-guard.

From my willingness to take another man into my bed to the post-coital confession that confirmed our romp had to be a one-time deal, the whole encounter had me backpedaling. I'd replayed the whole night—in sordid detail—for myself every night before bed, drinking one of the beers from the second six-pack each time. The crisp flavor of hops was a pale comparison to the deliciousness that was Rowan himself, but the taste of the memory was the only thing I'd get.

A one-time thing.

Fucking stupid. Stupid to say it and stupid to pretend once would be enough.

Thankfully, the sound of Jack's car horn from my driveway blared loud enough for the whole block to hear, signaling my ride to dinner had finally arrived. I checked my pockets for my wallet, phone, and keys, then locked up and headed out.

"Took you long enough," I grumbled, sinking into the passenger seat of his car.

Jack rolled his eyes, loosening the knot on his tie. "Some of us have real jobs, Gil. Jobs that require us to go into an office every day and sit in traffic in order to leave."

"Sounds miserable."

"You're telling me." He threw the car into reverse and backed out, shifted to drive, and took off toward the middle of town. "Are you good with Francelli's?"

My stomach growled its approval before I could speak.

"You know I'll never say no to pasta and wine," I answered, stretching out my legs as far as the small space in Jack's car allowed. "I've been drinking through this shitty six-pack my new neighbor brought me on Sunday and I could use a change."

"Something from Top Hops?" Jack laughed.

"Yeah, but once he realized how bad it was, he picked something up from the liquor store instead."

Jack threw a quick glance across the console at me, eyes narrowed. "That's a weird way to welcome himself to the neighborhood."

"I fixed his kids bike earlier in the day," I explained. "Whatever you're trying to make it into, it's not that."

He made a contemplative sound, and I cranked up the radio to drown out whatever smart comment he'd been planning to make next. It wasn't an admission of guilt, but it wasn't an acquittal either. To my relief, though, by the time we got to Francelli's, Jack had decided to tell me a story about one of his co-workers and the possible affair they were having with the head of HR. It was mundane and predictable, exactly the kind of thing I needed in the wake of my poorly thought-out and libido-driven Sunday night fuck fest.

He was still rambling while we got seated in a booth, and going still when the waitress brought us a bottle of Chianti and two glasses. She poured a couple ounces into each, we ordered our usual—fettuccine for me and carbonara for Jack—and he was finally approaching the tail end of his story.

"And then we found out that it wasn't the fucking guy from IT who was banging Sheila. It was *his wife*!"

I made a face that I hoped conveyed shock. "You're kidding me."

Jack scoffed, sinking back against the red pleather booth and waving a dismissive hand in my direction.

"You're too isolated for your own good, Gil," he said, reaching for his wine. "That was top tier office gossip and it didn't even faze you."

"Even if I cared what other people did in their spare time, I wouldn't care who they fucked."

"Who someone is fucking is generally the most interesting thing about them," he protested, leaning forward more conspiratorially than before. "Which is why being your friend the past two years is so fucking boring."

I huffed, giving him the finger and pouring myself another glass of wine.

"Gil, come on." Jack took the glass out of my hand and threaded our fingers together, blinking across the table at me with eyes that looked far too much like his brother's. "I'm imploring you to please just go get laid one time."

"You're insane."

"I don't ask you for much," he protested, knocking my knuckles into the table.

"I'd do anything for you, Jack, but not tha—"

I was interrupted by a quiet voice from beside the table. "Hey, Gil."

Jack gave me a curious look before turning his head to the side, our hands still joined.

"Hey, Fisher," I said. "How's the bike holding up?"

"Good, thanks. I was meaning to come by and ask if you cou—"

"Fish." Another interruption, another indecipherable look from Jack. I tried to pull my hand away from his, but he dug his nails into my palm, holding me down.

"I was saying hi to Gil," Fisher said.

Rowan came to a stop in front of our table, stumbling over his own feet and almost sending Fisher onto the floor. He looked...different from the other times I'd seen him. Dressed in creased navy chinos and a short0-sleeved button-up tucked in with a brown belt and matching shoes, a floral bowtie perfectly centered over the dip of his throat. It was impossible to not remember the way he gasped for air and swallowed hard after I pushed the whole length of my cock inside of him.

"Gil," Rowan said, cheeks flushing beneath this constellation of freckles.

"Rowan." I tried again to get my hand away from Jack, who finally let up. "Good to see you again."

"Gil's trying to have dinner, Fish," Rowan said, placing both of his hands on Fisher's shoulders and turning him away from the table. "We should leave him and his…friend."

"Friend," Jack repeated, tilting his head to the side.

"This is Jack," I said, pointing at my asshole best friend who looked like he'd just eaten a canary. "This is my new neighbor, Rowan, and his son, Fisher."

Rowan wiped his palm on the front of his pants and reached over Fisher's head to shake Jack's hand. Jack returned the gesture, then took a drink of his wine.

"Nice to meet you," Rowan said, glancing nervously between Jack and me. "We didn't mean to interrupt."

"I wasn't interrupting," Fisher protested, adjusting the headphones in his ears with a heavy eye roll. "I was saying hello."

"Good to see you too, Fisher." I chuckled, lifting my wine up to my mouth as Fisher stalked away from the table. "Looks like you have an escapee on your hands."

"I…he…" Rowan launched into more of his adorable stuttering before he tugged the end of his bowtie and managed to get himself together. "Nice to meet you, Jack. Good to see you, Gil."

I tilted my head to the side to watch him go, scratching the side of my nose to cover my smile. The two of them took a seat at a booth across the restaurant, thankfully out of my line of sight. When I turned my stare back to Jack, he was watching me with a smug expression on his face and a threat in his eyes.

"You're fucking him," he said, clapping his hands.

"I'm having dinner with you," I corrected.

"You can beat around the bush all you want, Gil Valentine, but I know you've been inside of that man before."

I groaned, covering my face with my hands and working my fingers back into my hair. The scar across my eye pulled against my grimace, the skin feeling tighter than normal and far more uncomfortable than I was used to. The waitress brought our food, and it was the smell of the house-made alfredo that had my hands falling—defeated—into my lap.

"It was one time," I conceded, giving my pasta, and not my best friend, my full attention.

"When?"

"Sunday."

"Why?"

"Because he felt so bad about the shitty beer," I lied.

Jack scoffed, winding a forkful of noodles around his fork and shoving them into his mouth.

"Why?" he asked again, a pea falling back onto his plate.

"Because I wanted to."

"He's nothing like Philip," Jack said.

I dropped my fork onto the table with a clatter. "Exactly."

"Shit." Jack exhaled heavily, half of the amusement leaving his face. "I know that's what I said, but that's not how I meant it."

"Don't dig a deeper hole; I'm begging you."

"I just—"

"I wasn't even thinking about your brother when I took him to bed, Jack," I assured my best friend.

"Of course you weren't."

I picked up my fork again.

"I really just didn't ever picture you going for a man like him," Jack went on, his tone dripping with renewed amusement.

"Like him how?" I managed a bite of my pasta, relieved to find that even though my world was certainly slanting on its axis, the meal tasted normal. "Short?"

"Redhead."

"Bowtie."

Jack licked his lips and let out a quiet sigh. "Single dad."

"Who says he's single?" I tried to crack a smile.

"You wife him up already, Gil?"

I shook my head and reached for my wine.

"He has a kid," Jack said. "Where's the mom?"

"Dead," I answered.

He made an apologetic sound, and I threw a look up to the ceiling.

"It was a one-off," I said, hoping that was the truth. "He brought some shitty beer over after I helped Fisher with his bike and one thing just led to another."

I didn't need to tell Jack that I'd been Rowan's first time with a man. I didn't need to tell him how gorgeous Rowan looked when he was spread open and begging. None of that was anyone's business besides my own.

"Why just once?" he asked.

"You're not going to let this go, are you?"

He shook his head and topped off both our wine glasses.

"He has a fucking kid," I said. "And I'm not exactly step-dad material."

"No one says you have to marry the guy." Jack finished working loose the knot on his tie until it hung open and loose in the middle of his chest. He was getting ready to go in for the kill—I knew the signs. "Just take him to bed a few times until you get the gears turning again."

"You can't be serious right now."

"You're just out of practice."

"Jack. Are you listening to yourself?" I set my fork down again, the flavor still fresh in my mouth, but my appetite gone entirely.

"It makes me happy to see you getting back in the saddle is all," he said, smiling.

"I need you to relax on the metaphors."

"Grease the wheels," he said.

I clenched my molars together.

"Knock boots in the hay," he said next.

"You're getting confused."

"Netflix and chill."

The worst part of the whole thing was I knew Jack meant well. He'd seen me through some of the worst parts of my split with his brother and, in his opinion, a return to dating was a return to normalcy. It was something we'd never seen eye to eye on, but it wasn't anything worth fighting over either. His friendship was the most important thing in my life, and I wasn't going to risk it over something as skewed as a conflict of views about sex and dating.

I finished the rest of my wine and flagged down the waitress for another bottle and a box. That earned a sharp laugh from Jack, who finally relented and dug into his carbonara with as much gusto as he undoubtedly imagined me digging into Rowan with. Thankfully, he hadn't seen just how much purpose I'd demonstrated when Rowan had been the feast.

Another secret meant just for me and not my nosy best friend.

I made it through the rest of dinner with minimal jabs, but on the way home, I had Jack stop at the liquor store. I picked up a six-pack of the best beer they carried and brought it home with me. If Jack had any suspicions about why I was buying it, he didn't voice them. He told me goodnight, promised to see me soon, and headed back home.

I set the six-pack of beer on my kitchen counter, trying to decide what to do about Rowan Verne.

CHAPTER 9
ROWAN

"Will you take those things out of your ears and listen, please, Fisher."

Fisher rolled his eyes at me, another thing I wasn't fond of, but I tried to remember to choose my battles. If getting away with a couple of eye rolls made him more willing to at least pretend to listen to me, I'd call it a win.

"It's early."

"You have school in a week and you've been up late all summer. You need to get on a proper schedule."

Fisher stared at me, saying nothing. It was something his mom used to do whenever she didn't like what I said. Fisher might have inherited my hair and my freckles, but he'd gotten her eyes and the set of her jaw. Her stubborn streak too.

"It's early though."

I pinched the bridge of my nose and took a breath. "I'm aware of the time. That's the point."

"I'm not tired." Fisher crossed his arms over his chest.

"Because you've been staying up late and sleeping in."

"I'm just going to lie awake half the night."

Somehow, I doubted that, but I didn't want to get into a huge fight over something as silly as bedtime. "Fisher, please. I know the end of summer means a new school, and that's probably at least part of what has you all worked up, but you need to get back into a proper sleep routine."

"I hate it here." Fisher stormed away and up the stairs, his heavy footsteps booming through the house to voice his displeasure with me. He'd been surly all night, ever since we ran into Gil before dinner and I'd told Fisher not to interrupt him.

Though I remembered what it was like to be twelve and starting a new school, I followed Fisher up the stairs and to his room. The lights were off and his room was oddly silent, but I knew he was in there.

"Fisher, we don't leave the room angry, remember?" It was something I couldn't handle. Even now, years later, it still twisted my stomach into knots. It was better than it had been after the accident first happened, but it still stuck with me.

The worst of it was that I couldn't remember how the argument started, but it had snowballed because both Lisa and I could be hardheaded about things. The whole thing got blown out of proportion and the next thing I knew, she snatched her keys off the counter and told me she was going to see her mom. The door slammed behind her. Her tires squawked on the pavement when she pulled away. And that's the last thing I ever heard of her.

They found her car at the bottom of a ravine on the way to her mom's house. Her parents lived out of town, but the route was familiar to Lisa and she'd often said she could make the trip blindfolded.

"Fish?"

I stepped into the room and Fisher let out a sigh.

"Sorry, Dad."

"It's okay. You don't need to apologize. I get it. Do you want to talk about it?"

"Nah. I'm fine."

I lingered in the door for another half a minute, wondering where the time had gone. It seemed like only two weeks ago Fisher was born. Last week, he'd been a toddler. Now he was a grumpy pre-teen who didn't think he needed to do things like go to bed at a decent hour.

"Night, Fish."

"Night, Dad."

Satisfied that Fisher and I were back on good terms, I went downstairs. We'd managed to finish unpacking and the boxes had been collapsed and taken into the garage. For the moment, there was nothing for me to do. The house was livable, if not perfect. But perfection took time.

I stretched out on the couch and flicked the TV on. I missed having someone to watch TV with. It was stupid, but I liked talking about the shows I watched. I missed curling up with someone and choosing a show. I found a low-stakes reality show that was easy to follow, even if I forgot to pay attention sometimes.

I must have drifted off, but the sound of someone

knocking on my door had me getting to my feet. Shuffling across the living room, I looked at the time and realized it was nearly midnight. Fisher's shoes were still by the door, so he was still upstairs sleeping. My panic calmed further when I pulled the door open and saw Gil on my front step with a six-pack in his hand.

"I woke you." Gil looked apologetic. "Sorry, I saw lights on. I figured you were awake."

Stepping aside, I waved for him to come in. "I sat down for a minute and the next thing I knew, you were knocking on the door."

Gil hesitated in the doorway. "I can come back."

That was the last thing I wanted. Not because I didn't want him here, but because I did. He was all I'd been able to think about ever since the other night when I'd made an ass of myself. We said it was supposed to be a one-time thing, but here he was on my doorstep in the middle of the night with a six-pack of beer. A different brand from before.

"Is that your usual?" I asked him once he finally stepped inside. Gil tugged at one of the cans and handed it to me. I tried not to stare at his hands, but I had a weakness for hands like Gil's. Long fingers. Tight grip. The kind that still had me feeling his touch days later.

"Figured it was my turn." Gil's gaze took in the decor as he toed out of his shoes. The walls needed a coat of paint, and some of the fixtures were in desperate need of updating, but I doubted Gil cared much about things like that.

I wanted to ask him what he was doing here, but my mouth had gone dry and my ability to form words had vanished, so I cracked open the beer and took a drink. It had a lighter flavor than the last one we'd shared and it went down smooth.

"What episode is this?" Gil set the beer down on the table and took a seat on the couch.

"I don't know. I started the new season a couple hours ago, but I don't think I made it very far before I fell asleep."

Gil snagged the remote off the coffee table and clicked the show back to the first episode. "I've seen them, but they're good to re-watch."

His gaze flicked to me, standing awkwardly in my own home, then to the couch. "Have a seat, Rowan. I don't bite."

"That's a shame." My jaw dropped and I scrambled to recover, but Gil's eyes twinkled and he grinned at me like I'd said the right thing instead of the wrong one. From the heat of my face, I could tell I was blushing, which I hated. But with Gil looking at me expectantly, I couldn't just keep standing there. I managed to sit down on the other end of the couch without tripping over my own feet or further making an ass of myself.

A smile tugged at Gil's face, then he looked away from me and back at the television, giving me a perfect view at the scar that traveled down the side of his face.

"How did you get the scar?" I took another sip of the beer, more to stop myself from blathering on at him. Sometimes I thought I should be banned from speaking to attractive people. Clearly, I was terrible at it.

"An accident." Gil said.

"Does it still hurt?" My fingers twitched with the urge to touch it. I wanted to trace the ruined skin with my fingertips and explain to him that the scar was probably the hottest thing I'd ever seen. But that was probably weird. Amazingly, I was able to keep that particular thought on lockdown.

"Not anymore. Not often." Gil stretched an arm over the back of the couch, then looked over at me. His body was angled toward mine, and the way he held himself made me feel like prey that had wandered directly into the path of the predator. Instead of running, though, it made me want to roll over and surrender.

"What are you doing here, Gil?" I didn't move when he dragged his gaze down my body, appraising me. Maybe remembering the same things I'd been remembering for the past three days.

"Where's Fisher?" Gil's voice was darker now, huskier. Hungrier.

"Upstairs. Asleep."

I swallowed audibly. "We said… one time."

My mouth needed to stop moving, unless it was against his mouth. Or some other equally appetizing part of his anatomy.

"That's what we said," Gil agreed. Then he leaned forward, somehow encroaching into my space, trapping me with the intensity of his stare. "Is that what you want?"

"Not especially."

"God, Rowan, you…"

I might never know how Gil intended to finish that sentence because his mouth was on mine, hand in my hair at first, then around the back of my neck to keep me where he wanted me. As if I intended on going anywhere. As if there were any place on the planet I'd want to be rather than right here. Except maybe closer to Gil.

Tentatively, I reached for him, running my hand up his arm. His skin was hot and the t-shirt he wore was impossibly soft, a stark contrast to the rough stubble on his cheeks. Gil kissed me like he'd die if he stopped. Like his life depended on mapping the inside of my mouth with his tongue. And I was powerless against him. I had no defenses against a man like him—all tall, dark, and broody. For a minute earlier today, I thought he was on a date and my stomach had sunk down to the bottom of my feet, taking my heart with it. But they were friends. And Gil and I were—something else.

Reaching for Gil with my other hand proved to be a mistake because I forgot I was holding on to a beer. The can dropped from my hand, landing on my lap. The cold liquid made me gasp and I pulled away, snatching the can off my lap before it could make a bigger mess.

"Fuck." I shot to my feet and tugged at the saturated fabric of my pants. "That was smooth, Rowan. Real smooth."

Gil rose to his feet, seemingly unbothered by my flightiness. It was like I was always flustered around him and he just didn't care. He didn't look at me weird, or make an excuse to leave. He just pretended it was normal for me to act unhinged all the time.

"If you wanted out of your pants, all you had to do was say so." Gil set his beer down and reached for me. Before I could say no, he hauled me against him, wrapping one arm around my waist while he popped the button of my pants open effortlessly.

Gil handled me like he knew me better than I knew myself. The possibility that he just might left me feeling vulnerable, but not to the point where I shut down. No, instead I came alive, whimpering into Gil's mouth when he worked his hand into the front of my pants.

There wasn't a single thing about Gil that was hesitant. The fact that he knew exactly what he wanted to do to me turned me on more than anything I'd ever experienced. He tugged me slowly, but with a possessive grip that made my eyes roll into the back of my head.

It wasn't the motorcycle or the scar on Gil's face that made him dangerous. It was the way I craved his touch. The way I melted when he kissed me. It was the way I wanted him to have me however he'd take me, however he wanted me. I barely knew him, but that didn't seem to matter because I doubted I'd be able to stay away from him.

Gil stroked me again and I let out an embarrassingly loud moan which was answered by Gil's mouth sealing over mine, muffling the sound.

"Shhh," he said. "You need to be quiet for me, Rowan. Can you do that?"

His thumb slid over the sensitive head of my cock, swiping at a bead of precum that had leaked out. I bit my lip and stifled another sound.

"That's good, Rowan. Just like that."

I was too turned on to be embarrassed by the way my cock leaked with every word Gil spoke. The praise he gave me sent frissons of pleasure arcing through my body. My brain and my dick agreed that I liked being told I was good. Later maybe I'd have the brainpower to unravel that particular revelation, but for now, all I could manage to do was wrap my arms around Gil's neck and let him devour me.

CHAPTER 10
GIL

Shoving Rowan's pants down to his knees was a bad idea. Curling my fingers around his cock and stroking him until precum smeared across the palm of my hand was even worse. Knowing and caring weren't the same thing, and knowing wasn't enough to stop me from doing the latter over and over and over again until I had to clamp my hand over his mouth so he didn't wake up his kid.

Fuck.

His *kid*.

What was I doing fucking around with a single dad who had a sleeping pre-teen upstairs? One with Rowan was already one time too many for me, and here I was, back for more, knowing full well he carried the biggest and reddest flag any man ever could. I didn't want kids, mine or someone else's, and having a repeat with Rowan—even with no commitment between us—was way too close to kids for comfort. Rowan's dick throbbing in my hand was enough to make me temporarily forget that, though, and soon my own cock was just as hard as his.

Dragging my hand away from his mouth and letting it rest on his throat, I let my lips hover over his, the promise of a kiss almost too much to bear. Rowan reached forward with his whole body, pressing his throat into my hand, his lips against mine. Suddenly, the bottle of lube I'd stashed in my pocket before coming over didn't seem like such a silly idea. I hadn't bothered with getting condoms when Jack had run me by the liquor store, but that was a conversation Rowan and I still needed to have at some point. Ideally with clothes on and no beer in our throats.

"I can't date you," I whispered, still touching Rowan in all the places that mattered the most. "I won't."

"Whatever."

Rowan was too new, too inexperienced.

With all the regret I could muster, I pried myself away from his cock and took a deep breath.

"It's not whatever," I said, squinting down at him with narrowed eyes. "I'm being serious."

"I'm not looking to date anyone," he said, yanking up his pants. His expression bordered on angry, hands shaking as he tried to pull up on his zipper. "You don't have to worry."

"Don't be like that, Row." I cocked my head to the side and frowned at him.

"I'm not like anything," he argued, still fighting his fly. "This is just...I'm how I am."

I knew that about him already. I understood the way Rowan was and I liked it, but I definitely wasn't going to tell him that.

"I'm trying to have an adult conversation with you about adult things."

Something about those words seemed to sober him, and he gave up on his pants, leaning against the back of the couch and scrubbing both hands down his face with a groan. "I know. I'm sorry."

"Why don't you go change into clothes that aren't soaked in beer and we can finish this conversation once you're dry?"

Rowan huffed a breath out his nose like a bull. "Are you telling me what to do?"

Heat surged between my legs. "Would you like that?"

He cursed under his breath and shook his head. "I'll go change."

Rowan walked off without another word and I found myself alone in Rowan's house for the first time. The place had definitely seen better days, run down by time after Carl McAllister's death, but even after a handful of days, Rowan was already managing to bring some life back into the property. His furniture was nice enough, not new but not old, worn and loved in all the right places. The living room definitely needed a coat of paint and the TV must have been almost a decade old, but it was all very *Rowan*, in a way I couldn't articulate. It was going to take a lot of hard work and elbow grease to turn the place from a house back into a home, though, and Rowan was only one man.

One man with a fucking kid.

Rowan returned with bare feet and gray sweatpants, which felt inherently unfair. He was smaller than me in every way, but his cock was still hard, tenting against the soft material and begging to be seen. He'd covered his upper body with a plain white undershirt that looked to be right out of the package, but closer inspection revealed Rowan was simply the kind of man who washed his whites in hot water with bleach.

Of course he was.

The memory of his perfectly knotted bowtie was still too fresh in my mind for him to be anything but a man who had crisp white undershirts with hems that weren't frayed. He couldn't have been more my opposite.

Another red flag.

I'd learned that lesson already.

Rowan cleared his throat and I blinked quickly, tearing my stare away from the bulge between his legs to look him in the eye. I shouldn't have come over. I knew that without being told, but I couldn't stay away from him. I wanted him. Wanted him more than I'd wanted anyone or anything in a considerable amount of time.

"I'm changed," he said, shrugging and sort of throwing his arms out to his sides.

"You are."

"What did you want to talk about?"

Rowan, even with his dick hard, was guarded and more defensive than he'd ever been. It was the same fear I saw when he chased down Fisher in my driveway the first day we'd met. That concern and uncertainty manifesting into something combustible and dangerous if stoked.

"This was supposed to be a one-off," I reminded him.

I hadn't moved from behind his couch, and Rowan joined me there again, leaning against the back of the couch and folding his arms in front of his chest, which only confirmed my earlier assessment of his mood.

"And you're back for more," he taunted.

I licked my lips, pulling them in between my teeth and biting down to stop myself from offering to leave. He wasn't wrong. I'd seen the way he stared so hard at Jack's and my joined hands, felt the jealousy rolling off of him in waves. And even still, I'd stopped at the store and bought beer. I'd taken it home, I'd thought better of the whole thing, and still. *Still*, I'd pocketed a bottle of lube and walked my happy ass around the block and knocked on his door.

"Maybe poor judgement on my part," I said, raising a brow. His glare tracked down the length of my scar before settling on my mouth. I released my lips, and his nostrils flared. "I can go."

"No!" Rowan surged forward, hands raised to stop me. He fell over his feet and slammed into me, palms hot and sweaty even through my shirt. I took a step backward to steady us both and grabbed him by the wrists to move us both back upright.

"No," he said again, softer.

"I can't offer you any more than I can offer."

"Gil, I…I don't…" Rowan stammered his way into another nervous monologue, and instead of being turned off, my traitorous dick thickened even more. "I don't know what I'm doing here. Even if I'd been with a man before, I haven't…haven't been with anyone since Lisa, and I don't know how to *not* be married anymore."

"I'm not the marrying type, Rowan."

"I mean, the whole casual thing. This isn't even casual, is it? It's not even a thing at all."

I puffed a long breath out, my cheeks deflating as I

exhaled my trepidation right into the shitty carpet that was no doubt on Rowan's list of things to address.

"It's not a thing at all," I confirmed.

"Not at all," he said softly.

Rowan had turned from defensive to defeated, even though both of our bodies were far from either of those feelings. A dark wet spot had appeared on the front of Rowan's sweats, and it took all my willpower to not fall to my knees to clean it up.

"More than once," Rowan continued, pausing to swallow. "Just not more than it is."

"Right," I agreed, taking a step toward him and hooking my finger over the waistband of his pants. "Did you wear these on purpose?"

His cheeks burned red.

"Rowan, you fucking kill me," I said, closing the rest of the space between us. He tilted his head back to look up at me and, damn, I loved the sight of him bent and angled to reach me. "I want to put my cock in your mouth so fucking much. Want to come in the back of your throat and make you choke on it."

Against me, he shivered.

"So, I guess this means you always talk like that," he rasped.

Reaching up, I traced the edge of my finger along his cheekbone, relishing the way his lashes fluttered at my touch.

"I do," I told him.

"I've never sucked a cock before," he said. "Sometimes I've used a toy, though."

The two sides of Rowan Verne were going to give me whiplash. I had no idea how he could be so obtuse and bumbling in one breath and so accidentally forward in the next. Like, when he was horny enough, he lost the ability to censor himself. And *fuck* if that wasn't the hottest thing ever. I loved being able to dismantle him like that, take him apart until he wasn't anything more than a quivering need...*for me*.

"What do you mean you've used a toy?"

"You know, like...in my mouth instead of in my—"

I covered his mouth again with my whole hand, fingers wrapping around toward his ear. "That's enough."

He was going to take me apart again before I even had a chance to get started. "How about I show you how I like it, and then you can try for yourself?"

"Show me how?"

The question died in his throat, because I went to my knees and took his sinful gray sweatpants with me. Rowan's hard cock bobbed in front of my face, as pink as the rest of him and slick around the tip with all the precum he'd been leaking while we talked. His balls were hot and heavy in my hand, and the sound that fell out of his mouth when I tested their weight was enough to make my own dick leak against my thigh.

"It's okay to tease sometimes," I said, pulling his cock against his stomach so I could mouth that sensitive swatch of skin where his shaft and balls were joined. With my tongue and my lips, I sucked him there until he was soaking wet, then slowly dragged my mouth up his length. "As long as you know when playtime is over."

He tasted like salt and soap, and when I sealed my lips around the tip of his cock, his entire body buckled in half. He folded over me with a strangled grunt, forcing himself all the way into my mouth whether I liked it or not. Thankfully, while still well-endowed, Rowan was shorter than me and skinnier than me in all of the ways possible.

Stretching my free hand up under his shirt, I pushed him back up so I could bob up and down his shaft, swirling my tongue and groaning quietly at the feel of him against the roof of my mouth. I took his hands and threaded his fingers into my hair, blinking up at him with a wall of unshed tears in my eyes. Humming around the base of his cock, I flattened my tongue against the underside of his shaft and sucked hard. It was all the sign he needed. Tightening his hold in my hair, Rowan's hips snapped forward and he came hard and fast right into the back of my throat.

CHAPTER 11
ROWAN

My knees would have buckled had I not been able to put some of my weight on Gil. I was at least eighty-nine percent sure that he'd actually sucked my brains out of my cock. In ten seconds flat, no less. The swiftness of my orgasm dawned on me and I let out a groan.

Gil pulled back, releasing my magically still hard cock from his mouth. He looked up at me, smug as hell. The side of his mouth curved up and he swiped at a stray drop of cum, tucking his finger into his mouth to suck it off.

The man was fucking obscene.

I should have been more insulted by the fact that he didn't want to date me, but it had hardly come as a shock. I knew what I looked like, what I acted like. I knew better than anyone how awkward I could be. Hardly a catch, especially for someone like Gil. Yeah, I'd seen it coming a mile away, but I had to admit that the amazing blow job took the sting out of the whole thing.

Hell, when I changed, I'd half expected him to be gone by the time I made it back to the living room. But he'd surprised me by his continued presence.

He rose to his feet, dragging his mouth up my skin as he went. Kissing my stomach, my chest, before nuzzling in against my neck, practically purring as his hands rested on my hips. The friction of Gil's jeans when he pressed himself against me was almost too much to handle.

I bit back a whimper and Gil's fingers dug into my bare hips as his lips brushed over mine. Gil's hunger was a feral thing, gnashing at me with sharp teeth. Grabbing at me and tugging me closer, he pressed me against the back of the couch. Being pinned there made my cock twitch. My breath caught and I found myself begging for more. Maybe it was the absolute lack of sex in my life, or maybe it was just Gil, but I'd gone from not caring about getting off to wanting to be under Gil as often as possible.

It's all I'd thought about for the past three days. In the shower. In the morning and at night. I'd tried to keep my mind off him by throwing myself into project after project, but he was never far from my mind.

I felt like I dreamed him.

He kissed me deeper, silencing the whimpers that had started to pour out of me when he pinned me to the back of the couch.

"Shhh," Gil kissed the corner of my mouth. Stubble scratched against my cheek as he dragged his talented mouth down the line of my jaw. His fingers delved between my cheeks and I sucked in a breath. From his pocket, he retrieved a bottle of lube and I didn't stop to think about how presumptuous that was. Or how hot it made me.

Gil set the lube on the back of the couch and yanked his pants open. One day soon, I wanted to put my mouth on him, but he gripped my hips and flipped me around so my front was pressed into the couch. He skimmed a hand down my back and over the globes of my ass, then freed his cock from his pants by shoving them down to mid-thigh.

Time slowed and I watched him slick his fingers with lube before sliding up closer to me. "You need to be quiet, Row. Can you do that?"

Breathless without even being touched, I nodded. The truth of it was that I'd probably do anything Gil asked of me. My eyes reflexively shut when he pressed a finger against my hole, circled it with a touch that was too possessive to be gentle, but delicious all the same.

He entered me slowly with that finger, sliding in and out a few times before he cupped my cheek with his other hand. His mouth crashed down over mine as he inserted a second finger in. For a long, blissful moment, I was unable to do anything but breathe and concentrate on opening myself to him. Then suddenly it was like I came alive. Like he'd breathed me into existence again. I writhed on his hand, fucking myself on his fingers, not caring how needy I must have looked. How desperate I must have sounded.

Gil let out a quiet, but frustrated sounding grunt and pulled away.

"Can you keep quiet or do I have to help you?"

I watched, mesmerized by the way he handled his cock, applying a generous amount of lube.

"How would you help me?" Without his touch, I felt unmoored and a little self-conscious standing in the middle of my living room with my bare ass hanging out and my pants around my feet.

Gil stepped up behind me. His mouth connected with my shoulder, the nape of my neck. One hand anchored on my hip, the other he used to guide his cock to my waiting hole. The blunt end pressed against me, but didn't go any further.

"Yes or no, Rowan." Gil said.

"Yes," I said.

The answer would always be yes. I was weak for him. For any scrap of attention he'd throw my way. Even if he didn't want to date me, he wanted me—at least for this. And I'd take what I could get.

Gil's cock glided forward, stretched the ring of tender skin and muscle slowly to accommodate the intrusion. I gripped onto the back of the couch with both hands and arched my back as his teeth scraped at my skin. Sharp incisors on tender flesh made my head swim.

Whatever I'd expected from Gil, it wasn't this raw intensity or the languid pace at which he fucked me. Every inch of him slid into me like it belonged there. He buried his face against the back of my neck, hot breath washing over my skin. And he kept going at that slow, sweet pace.

"Gil, I—" My words cut off into a moan and suddenly his hand was over my mouth, his breath in my ear. Our bodies so close you couldn't slot a sheet of paper between us.

"Quiet, Rowan." He reached around and took my cock in his hand. I was powerless to do anything but stand there and be ruled by him. My brain didn't know what sensation it liked the most. The hand on my mouth. The one on my cock. Or the way he filled me.

Gil's speed didn't increase. He fucked me in slow, deep thrusts. He didn't jerk me off either, but instead squeezed the base of my cock when I got too close to the edge. Time lost meaning. I was a sweaty mess of a man, melted in Gil's arms, my whimpers met with quiet reminders to keep my voice down.

The intensity made my head spin. It might have been the lack of oxygen or blood flow to my brain. Then… Gil's pace picked up. He was taller than I was and every so often he'd fuck me deeper, like he was rising up on his toes to see how far inside me he could get.

If he asked, I'd have told him he was everywhere. Under my skin and in my bones. My blood. But he didn't ask. Instead his hand on my mouth clamped tighter and his other started moving, using my precum to smooth the glide of his fingers on my cock. All I could do was hold on.

"Fuck, Row. So good for me, aren't you?"

Praise from Gil had a way of undoing me. It was stupid, but I wanted him to like me.

He turned my head and moved his hand only to replace it with his mouth. My body was light and tingly except for the pulse of impending orgasm between my legs and the fire that burned in my veins. He kissed me deeper as I started to come, coating his hand with my release. I wanted to reach for him, but I couldn't in the position I was in.

For as quiet and slow as he'd fucked me, his orgasm was no less intense than the first one. He fucked me until he was at the precipice, then pulled out. The loss I felt was the thing that made me nearly crumple to the floor, but Gil held me steady with an arm around my waist. He jerked behind me, the sound of skin on skin not unfamiliar to me. I felt something warm hit my back, then my ass.

"Fuck," His voice shook. Fingers smeared the mess around on my skin and then those same fingers were pressed between my lips and into my mouth. "I wanted to come inside you last time. And this time too. Wanted to fill you and watch it leak out of you, but I wanted you to taste me too."

It was salty and not unpleasant and I licked my lips when Gil's fingers retreated from my mouth. "I have a feeling it would be better direct from the source."

Gil groaned and ground his flagging erection against me. He gripped my hips again and pressed his forehead between my shoulder blades. My legs quaked and the cum drying on my ass wasn't ideal for comfort, but I couldn't bear to move. Not yet.

"Will you? Next time?"

Gil chuckled behind me. "Full sentences, Row. Gonna need some context."

"Come inside me. Next time. You're the only one I've been with since—in a long time."

If there would be a next time. There wasn't supposed to have been a second time. Would Gil really be interested in me for a third round? I tried not to let that thought depress me. The fact that I only had a few days left before returning to work was already weighing on me. A new office in a new city with new colleagues. I know I'd moved for a fresh start, but that didn't mean starting over was all fun and games.

"Would you like that?" The husky quality of Gil's voice dragged me back into the present. He ran his hands over my skin, up under my shirt and wrapped his arms around me. Just as I started to wonder if Gil was a secret snuggler after sex, he was gone.

He bent over and pulled my sweats up my legs and over my ass. By the time I managed to turn around, he was tucked back in his pants. He yanked the zipper up and I couldn't help but lean in and steal a kiss.

He didn't want to date me. That was fine. But maybe we could be friends. Friends kissed sometimes. Friends fucked sometimes. But I didn't know how to ask for that without making him think I wanted more.

"I would like that, for the record," I answered finally.

Gil smirked at me, his smile always slightly crooked because of the scarring on his face. But his imperfections only added to his appeal.

Taking a chance, I took another step toward him and tilted my head up to look him in the eyes. Our mouths were just a breath apart. "I'd like that a lot," I told him before stealing another kiss that tasted like both of us.

When we parted, Gil looked at me, his gaze intense in a way I couldn't read. "Never wipe my cum off again, Rowan."

I wasn't sure what he was referring to, but I smiled and agreed, resting my hands against his chest.

"Never," I promised.

CHAPTER 12
GIL

'd been inside of him twice since I met him, but I didn't have Rowan's phone number. That was better, because I didn't need his phone number. What even would I do with it? We weren't boyfriends and we definitely weren't dating. We were just two neighbors who'd fallen into bed a couple of times. A couple times too many, but we'd somehow agreed that was maybe an okay thing and we didn't have to stop.

But I hadn't seen him since.

I'd been a good little Boy Scout, marching myself down to the clinic on Thursday to get swabbed, hoping Rowan would be responsible enough to do the same. It was bad enough we'd gone without condoms twice. Even though I hadn't come inside of him, I'd wanted it like air, the need to sink deep and paint his insides almost as urgent as my next breath. The first time he'd wiped my cum on the sheets, the second time, I fed it straight into his mouth to make sure it didn't go to waste.

The third time…if we ever had one…

I knew exactly where it was going to go.

After our quick fuck on Wednesday, I got dressed and took myself back home. Not even the crisp night air had been enough to cool the hear burning just beneath the surface of my skin. When I got back to my house, I jerked off in the shower, coming so hard I saw stars against the ceiling. After, I dried off and climbed into bed, ignoring the slew of text messages Jack had sent me after dropping me off at home earlier in the night.

> **JACK**
>
> It makes me happy to see you happy.
>
> I bet he's wild in the sack, isn't he?
>
> Actually, I don't want to know because that means I'd know what YOU are like in bed and by extension I'd know what my brother is like in bed and I don't want that.
>
> Sorry again. I don't mean to always bring him up.
>
> I hope you're fucking your step-kid's dad and not mad at me for what I said.
>
> Bet you're mad about that, though.

I exhaled heavily, rolling my eyes as if Jack were there to see me. He'd always been so good about not bringing up Philip, but the past two weeks I'd heard my ex's name more than I had in the past two years. There had to be a reason for it, but Jack hadn't mentioned anything, and I was never one to pry. Unsure of what to do with that line of thought, I filed it away for future-Gil to deal with, then promptly closed my eyes and fell asleep.

I slept hard and long, no dreams and no interruptions until an incessant banging from somewhere in my house pulled me back to consciousness. I blinked slowly, rubbing my eyes and rolling onto my side to check the time on my phone. It was barely eight in the morning, and the banging was someone pounding on my front door. If Rowan was coming to get laid, we were going to have to set some boundaries about his sense of time because, while I didn't think I had it in me to turn him away, I definitely wasn't going to perform to my best standards before I'd ever had caffeine.

The fist against my door stopped, and I flopped back onto my pillow, but before my eyes could close, it started up again.

"I'm coming!" I shouted, flinging my legs off the side of the bed and pushing to my feet.

On second thought, I definitely would *not* fuck Rowan after this kind of wake-up. Jack would have called if he wanted to pester me, so short of a political canvasser, I had no idea who needed me so urgently and so very fucking early on a Saturday morning. Grabbing a pair of shorts from the top of my hamper, I managed to get my lower half covered before yanking open the front door.

"What?" I answered, gruff and angry, finding no one at eye level to direct my anger at.

"Hey, you're awake."

The voice was soft and uneven in tone, and I looked down to find Fisher on my porch, his bike on its side, half on the concrete and half in my planter.

"I am now."

"My thing came loose again." He kicked at his bike.

I scrubbed a hand down my face and closed my eyes before rolling them so he didn't see. "The caliper?"

"Yeah, that's the word. I couldn't remember."

"I taught you how to fix it the first time," I reminded him, pointing around the corner of my house to the garage. "We were right in there, and I talked you through the whole thing."

"My dad doesn't have an Andrew wrench."

"Allen wrench," I corrected.

"That one." Fisher fussed with the buds in his ears.

"Are those on?" I asked.

He shook his head.

"Then take them out."

A flash of teenage defiance lit up his features, and then both white buds were tucked into his front right pocket.

"Can I borrow your Allen wrench?"

"Do you also need my garage?" I asked, tilting my head to the side. "And my spray grease?"

"My dad doesn't have the grease."

"Does your dad know you're here?"

"No."

I sighed. "I'll open the garage up, but I haven't even had coffee yet, so you're on your own."

"Thanks, Gil."

I closed the front door in his face, went down the hallway to open the exterior garage door, then shuffled into the kitchen to make some coffee. Mercifully, it brewed quickly, and I got a shirt while the carafe filled to the brim. Pouring myself a mug, I headed toward the garage, somehow not surprised in the least to find Fisher with his dirty hands all over the fuel tank of my bike instead of the brakes on his own.

"She doesn't need any grease," I said.

He started and stumbled backward, tripping over his bike and falling into the fender of my Cougar. Thankfully, like most things in my life, the car needed a lot of work and not even the force of Fisher's bony hip would be enough to take her down.

"Your bike is cool," he said, righting himself and turning to his bicycle.

"I know."

Leaning against my toolbox, I sipped my coffee while Fisher sank down onto his knees to get at the brake caliper on his bike. He'd at least paid attention the first time I went through it with him, and I watched while a quickly growing sense of pride spread outward from the middle of my chest. Rubbing my sternum, I chased the feelings down with a drink of coffee that was far too big and still far too hot.

"I've always wanted one when I get old enough to get my license," Fisher said, trying to make conversation.

"Absolutely not," I snapped at him, like I had any place to dictate what he could or could not do. Clearing my throat, I lowered my tone. "I mean, that's up to your dad."

"He won't let me."

"Good."

Fisher shot daggers at me with his eyes. "I'll just get one when I turn eighteen."

"With what money?" I asked.

"I'll get a job."

"And the insurance?"

"I said I'll get a job." Fisher's cheeks were a dark and angry kind of red, not from a real sense of anger, but the kind that came with being called out for not knowing better. I was familiar with the feeling, and the shame that came with it.

For months after my accident, I'd carried the same feeling around like a weight on my shoulders. Except I *should* have known better. I'd been riding long enough to know the conditions were not ideal and my speed was excessive. There was an old saying about riding—*It's not if you crash, but when.* My *when* had almost taken my life, and it was a long time before I'd had the courage to get back on two wheels. But once I did, all the fear over my near-miss evaporated into thin air.

Fisher had either given up on the argument or gotten tired of it, maybe both. He didn't say anything beyond his protests about getting a job, but he set back to work on fixing the brakes on his bike. I settled back against my toolbox, drinking my coffee. Even though he'd woken me up far too loudly and far too early for the weekend, the weather outside was tolerable and his quiet company wasn't the worst.

For a kid, at least.

Maybe after Fisher finished up and took off, I'd go for a ride up to the mountains, get out of town for the day. The winter would be here sooner rather than later, and I wanted to take advantage of the few remaining nice days we had left. However, all thoughts of a peaceful weekend ride were interrupted when Jack's car pulled into my driveway.

He climbed out of his car with a cardboard drink carrier and crumpled bag of donuts balanced in one hand, his eyes dancing with amusement when he saw Fisher in the middle of my garage.

"What are you doing here?" I asked.

Fisher looked up, recognizing Jack from the night before, but not offering him a hello.

"You weren't answering my texts and I thought you were mad at me."

"Very friendly," Fisher muttered under his breath.

"Are you finished yet?" I asked him, eyebrow raised.

He stood at my question, dusting off his knees and taking the grease and the Allen wrench back to their place on top of my toolbox.

"I'm finished," he said quietly, pausing before asking, "Are you sure you're just friends?"

"Why do you care?"

"I heard you come over last night."

"So?" I tightened my hold on my coffee, knuckles turning white against the porcelain.

"Are you and my dad *friends* too?" The accusation in his words was thick, and it was clear I needed to have a talk with Rowan about where we fucked and how loud he got while it happened.

"It's not your business what me and your dad are." I pushed away from my toolbox and picked up his bike, rolling it into the driveway to help him along. "Have your dad buy an Allen wrench, Fisher."

"He's tearing up the floor in the bathroom," Fisher said with a shrug, hopping into his bike and riding down my driveway without another word. He turned left, standing on the pedals and giving the bike a little jump before speeding off and out of sight.

"Do you want to talk about what just happened?" Jack asked, mouth twisted into a knowing smirk.

I flipped him off and turned, heading back into my house to refill my coffee. Jack was hot on my heels with his Styrofoam cups, which he dumped one of into my mug before I could even get to the pot.

"I brought you a maple bar to soften the blow," he said.

"What blow?"

"Of my texts last night. I didn't mean to bring Philip up."

The sudden recurrence of my ex-boyfriend's name in my life that I'd filed into the darkest and most forgotten corner of my brain made its way back front and center, his stupid name blinking in marquee lights if I closed my eyes for too long.

"And yet you continue," I murmured.

"He's been…it's not your problem."

"But it's your problem," I said, nudging Jack out to the living room and down onto the couch. "And you're my best friend, so let's talk about it."

"You hate talking."

"I know."

"So why are we doing it?" he asked, brows furrowed.

"Because you need to."

"I don't want to," Jack protested weakly, shrugging. "I just…"

"Would you spit it out before I throw you out of my fucking house, Jack?"

"Philip's getting married," he blurted, eyes going wide. He shrank down into my couch like he wanted it to swallow him whole, and I had to admit I wished it would.

"Oh."

I didn't know what else to say, the shock was a paralytic, and it was only the burn of my palms against the outside of the mug that shocked me back into the present. There'd been a time Philip and I had talked about getting married. In fact, we'd talked about it often, but there'd been a deal breaker between us, and…loving Philip just wasn't enough anymore.

"He's getting married," Jack repeated, gnashing his molars together and facing me head on to deliver the next—nearly fatal—blow. "And he wants me to be his best man."

CHAPTER 13
ROWAN

Monday morning came and brought with it an air of disappointment. I'd half expected Gil to show up at my door again. I thought about going to his house with some manufactured excuse or another, but between getting Fisher ready for his first day, tearing up my bathroom floor, and dealing with a hot water tank that suddenly bit the bullet, my weekend had gotten away from me.

Taking a final glance at myself in the mirror, I straightened my bowtie, and smoothed down a flyaway hair that immediately sprang back out of place. I gave up on the hair and went to the kitchen.

Fisher stood in front of the coffee maker and poured two cups. One for me, one for him. Drinking coffee was a new thing he'd decided to do, probably to feel older. Though maybe he actually liked it. He took less sugar in his than I did in mine.

"Ready for your first day?" I asked.

Fisher cut me one of his signature surly teenager side-eyes.

"Right, sorry. Of course you're ready. You were born ready. Right, Fish?"

"Please, no small talk, Dad." Fisher took a sip of his coffee.

"I'm allowed to make small talk," I contested as I stirred a third spoonful of sugar into my coffee. "It's my job as your dad to be as cringe as possible."

Fisher wrinkled his nose. "Don't say cringe."

"Why not? Is it *cringe* when I say it?"

Fisher rolled his eyes and I mentally tallied up a point for me.

"Are you sure you don't want a ride?"

"I'll bike, thanks. By the way, Gil said you need to buy an Andrew—Allen wrench. My calipers keep coming loose."

"What's a—never mind. Find the one you need and send me a link and I'll order it."

Fisher mumbled something that I didn't catch, but I'd run out of time to interrogate him about it. Besides, I'd learned that some of his mumbles weren't meant for me.

"I have to run, but if you need me, I'll have my cell on."

Was I nervous about Fisher's first day at a new school in a new city? Absolutely. My nerves for his first day eclipsed the ones I had about my own. At least they had until I got in the car and backed out of the driveway. I went the long way around rather than pass by Gil's house.

In general, I liked what I did for a living. Was it glamorous? Not especially. There wasn't much glitz and glamor being a mortgage broker. But I was good at what I did and the firm I'd been transferred to was part of the same company I'd worked for back home. But their smaller offices were having trouble keeping people. The lure of big city living often drew people away.

Mosaic Mortgages was just off Main Street nestled between a little mom-and-pop style pizza place and a tattoo shop. We were situated just down from the banks, which occupied three out of four corners of an intersection. Employee parking was around back and I navigated the narrow alleyway to the lot behind the building. Jenny, the office manager, had told me to text her when I arrived and she'd let me in.

My phone pinged with a text. Fisher had sent me a selfie of himself outside his new school. The text that accompanied it said *proof of life*. Fisher wasn't smiling in the picture, but that wasn't unusual for him. My heart twisted at that and I sent a silent wish out into the universe. Maybe something would come along that would change that for him. I could only hope.

I sent my new boss Jenny a quick text, letting her know I was out back and I climbed out of the car with my messenger bag in hand. It had my work computer in it and though I hadn't touched it since I moved, it felt kind of nice to be getting into a proper routine again.

Jenny, despite the youthful name, turned out to be a woman pushing sixty with silver hair piled on top of her head in an artful, slightly messy bun. Her glasses were thick and a sparkly chain connected to each arm and ran behind her neck. She waved me inside and greeted me with a handshake. Jenny, even in heels, was at least a head shorter than I was.

"Rowan Verne, it's so good to meet you in person. I'll give you the grand tour and show you to your little corner of our office and let you get settled in before I feed you to the wolves."

"We have a lovely client base, Jenny. Don't listen to her." A deep voice had me turning my head. It belonged to a man who had long legs and a short, neatly trimmed beard.

"I was talking about you, Morgan. Morgan Sergeant, this is Rowan Verne, our newest broker. Don't scare him away."

Morgan put his hand over his heart. "You wound me, Jenny." He extended his hand toward me. "It's good to meet you, Rowan."

"Thanks."

"Don't listen to a word she says about me." Morgan pulled his hand away and tucked it in his pocket.

"It's all true," Jenny shot back with a smile.

"That's precisely why he shouldn't listen." Morgan threw me a grin, then turned his attention to Jenny. "Mel called out sick and she had a full schedule today."

"Fuck." Jenny cut a look to me and grimaced. "Sorry, I try to curb the potty talk, but this puts me in a tight spot."

"I might be new to the office, but I'm not new. I can probably get myself up to speed enough to tackle her schedule. It wasn't like I had much planned for today besides picking what side of the desk I want my stapler on." It was going to be a trial by fire, that was certain, but there was no better way to keep my mind off Fisher and his first day, and Gil and the fact that I hadn't seen him all weekend. The distraction was welcome.

"Can you get him set up and bring him up to speed on Mel's clients, and I'll give them a call and see if any want to reschedule?" Jenny didn't wait for him to answer before she disappeared around the corner.

"When Jenny gives an order, it might sound like a question, but it's not," Morgan offered, then motioned for me to follow him. "I'll give you the speed-run tour." Morgan was definitely younger than me. Maybe twenty-five or so. Maybe thirty with an amazing skin care routine.

When he said speed-run, he wasn't joking. The whole tour took about two minutes and I knew later I'd know where exactly nothing was. But then we were suddenly in my office. Before I transferred, I hadn't had an office. I had a glorified cubicle.

I no sooner sat down at my desk that Morgan fired up my computer. "Your work laptop will be good for when you're working from home, but you're not connected to this office yet. It'll be faster today if you use this." He brought up the main screen and then backed away. "Your username is your first and last name and your password is pineapple. You'll have to change that when you log in, but Jenny had me set you up in the system last week so you'd be ready to go."

I logged in and then Morgan showed me where to access Mel's cases. All the clients' information could be accessed by any of the brokers.

"It should be straight forward. I'll be right across the hall if you need anything. Or you can dial me directly by pressing the pound key, then eight-eight-seven. Jenny is five-five-four."

"And if things go really south, I can always dial nine-one-one."

Morgan cracked a smile and patted me on the back. His hand lingered on my shoulder for a second before he pulled it away. "I think you'll fit in just fine, Rowan. Welcome to Mosaic."

He knocked on the doorframe as he exited, which was weird when I thought about it. People usually knocked on their way into a room.

Pushing thoughts of anything else aside, I got to work.

Mel's schedule had been jammed, but Jenny managed to reschedule a couple appointments for the following day. I nearly worked through lunch, but Morgan stopped in with a calzone from the pizza place and an iced coffee. I didn't have the heart to tell him that I thought iced coffee was the devil. The fact that he'd thought of me was sweet.

By the time the workday wrapped up, I was dead on my feet and eager to hear from Fisher, who hadn't texted since his proof of life picture that morning. Jenny and Morgan caught up to me on my way out and she apologized for my first day being a shit show, then she apologized again for swearing. With a promise that tomorrow would be three hundred percent less hectic, she let Morgan and me go.

"How about a first day drink?" Morgan asked. "It's on me."

"Actually, I have to get home to my kid. His first day at a new school was today and I want to see how it went."

"You have a kid? How old?"

"Almost thirteen, going on twenty five. He's starting seventh grade."

"Is he an only child or do you and the missus have a whole herd of ankle-biters?"

"Just one. Uh… the missus is…" I grimaced whenever I had to tell people about Fisher's mom. "She passed away."

"Fuck. Sorry. Shit. Ah, right. So, you need to get home and I need to find a hole to crawl into." Pink climbed high on Morgan's cheeks, making his brown eyes stand out.

"That's not necessary, I promise."

Morgan ran a hand through his hair, making him look somewhat like a sheepish boy-next-door. "Maybe I can get a raincheck on that drink?"

"Maybe." I said, promising him nothing. "Thanks for lunch today, though."

Morgan beamed, flashing the hint of a dimple. "You're welcome."

It felt like it took an eternity to get home, and this time I didn't avoid driving past Gil's house. Not that it did any good. The garage door was shut and there was no sign of him outside. It made me feel slightly stalkerish when I realized I'd slowed down to gawk.

I wasn't obsessed. I was just… curious whether or not he'd fled the country to avoid me. He hadn't bothered to come over again after last time. And it shouldn't have bothered me, especially because I also hadn't drummed up the courage to go to his place.

Before I went inside, I walked to the mailbox at the end of the driveway and fished around inside for whatever had been delivered. The envelope wasn't addressed to anyone, but when I opened it, there was no mistaking that it was meant for me. A health clinic address was printed at the top, and below that was Gil's name and his sexual health test results.

Negative across the board.

The paper shook in my hand and I hastily shoved it back in the envelope. What did this mean? Did it mean he was done with me and just wanted me to know he hadn't put me at risk? Did it mean he wanted a repeat? It definitely meant that I should have also been tested and shame flooded me for not thinking of it sooner. I hadn't been with anyone since Lisa, though. Honestly, I didn't see the need, but it was what a responsible person would do.

First, I'd get my results, then I'd talk to Gil.

CHAPTER 14
GIL

Late Wednesday evening, my doorbell camera alerted to motion on the porch. I glanced at the alert on my phone, shoving my chair back from my desk to stretch. The day had really gotten away from me, and my eyes were bleary from how long I'd been focused on my screen. It had already been a rough week at work, with all kinds of things going wrong and I was the only person capable of putting out the fires. I was about an hour out from finishing what I hoped were the final corrective actions, but I definitely needed a break.

Before the Verne men had moved to town, I wasn't the type to get visitors. Jack came over often, but for the most part he was on a schedule, and he was also my best friend so the rules didn't quite apply to him. Fisher had been over more than his dad, but I found that neither of them were as unwelcome as they should have been. I was a solitary man and I enjoyed my peace and quiet. Fisher was anything but, and Rowan…well…he was something else entirely.

I knew one thing for certain, navigating out of my office and to the front door, it wasn't Jack on my porch. After seeing him on Saturday when he'd managed to drop two bombs in one go, he'd been scarce. Not ignoring me, but not as talkative as he usually was. His brother would always be a sore spot between us, but I didn't know which was more shocking. The fact Philip had asked Jack to be in his wedding or the fact he was getting married at all. A thousand questions about my ex's life tangled up in the back of my throat at Jack's confession, but I'd swallowed them all down. They would keep for another day when he didn't look so terrified of me. God knew what expression my face must have contorted into at the mention of Philip getting married.

Had he decided to settle down with a man or a woman? Did his intended have kids? Did they *want* kids? They'd have to, because there was no reason for it to have been our deal breaker for nothing.

Right?

Right?

Scrubbing a hand down my face, I pulled open my front door, half-expecting to see Fisher and his bike on my porch, but definitely not expecting to see Rowan, bent over with his ass in the air as he retrieved the keys he must have dropped. A white envelope stuck up out of his back pocket. He had on khaki pants that stretched across his ass in all the best ways, and I really did enjoy how proper he presented himself until I stripped him down to fuck.

"I normally like to do this kind of thing indoors," I said, leaning against the doorframe and crossing one ankle in front of the other. "But if you're into exhibition-ism, we can give it a try."

He started at the sound of my voice because of course he did, straightening up fast as a shot and almost falling over himself and into my grass. Rowan turned quickly and managed to regain his footing, showing me he had on a blue and white checkered button-up, short sleeves, with a blue floral bowtie collared neatly around his throat.

"I'm not," he said quickly, face as red as the roses around his neck.

I hummed. "That's a shame."

Rowan didn't say anything to that, so I cocked my head to the side and waited for him to announce himself.

Nothing.

"What brings you over this way, Rowan?" I asked, crossing my arms in front of my chest.

"I, uhm…I got your mail earlier this week."

I arched a brow. "My mail?"

"That you left for me, I mean."

Oh. My test results.

"Just being responsible after the fact since we weren't in the first place," I said.

"Right, of course." He reached into his back pocket and produced the white envelope, shoving it against my chest.

I reached for it before he could drop it, fingers grazing against his before he pulled away. I didn't antici-pate there being any surprises inside or Rowan would have been a lot more flustered than he was. A quick scan of the printout confirmed we were both clear to continue the way we'd started. A quick flash of arousal snaked up from the base of my spine, the mere thought of finally coming inside of him enough to almost send me over the edge.

"Where's Fisher?" I asked.

"Home," Rowan answered with a shrug. "Doing homework. I was going to pick up a pizza and wanted to come drop these off."

"How long do you have?"

Rowan's face somehow turned darker, and I realized my question must have sounded like a proposition.

"Not to fuck," I quickly corrected. "To talk."

Was it just me, or did he look crestfallen?

"I have five or ten until the pizza is ready," he said.

I gestured for him to follow after me, and then we were both alone in the entryway of my house, Rowan looking awkward as ever. This was new for us, I realized. Talking with clothes on had never been part of the spark between us, no matter how much we'd pretended to preface our sexual encounters with it. This was *just* talking, no promise of sex in sight.

"We've been fairly heat of the moment about things so far, and I just want to make sure we're on the same page," I explained.

He laughed nervously. "I'm just happy we're in the same book, but go on."

I wasn't sure what he meant by that, but I'd ask him another time.

"I'm not looking for a boyfriend," I told him.

"I know."

"And I'm not looking to be a dad. Step or otherwise."

Rowan opened his mouth like he wanted to speak,

but closed it before any words escaped. That was probably for the better.

"I'm not offering you anything more than what I already have," I said.

"Intimacy," he murmured.

"No." Rowan needed to get that idea out of his head immediately. "Sex."

"Same thing."

"No," I said again. "It's very much not."

I'd been intimate with Philip, just like Rowan had been intimate with his wife. You were intimate with partners, not neighbors you took to bed to pass the time.

"Okay," he said. "Are you…having sex with other people, then?"

"No."

"Are you intimate with anyone?" he asked me next.

"If I was, you wouldn't be here and we wouldn't be having this conversation."

Rowan grimaced, knotting his fingers together anxiously in front of his stomach like he didn't know what to do with his hands.

"You're the only person I'm doing *anything* with," I explained. "I would like to keep doing those things with you and I'd very much like to keep doing them without condoms, but if you're doing them with anyone else, if you're dating, if you're *intimate*—"

"I'm not," he said quickly, holding up his hands in surrender. "I'm not."

"You can if you want," I said. "I don't mind if you want to date other people, as long as they know about me."

About us.

"I'm not dating anyone," Rowan said quietly. "I don't have time, even if I wanted to. There's so much to do on the house and I'm getting settled at work, and Fisher starting his new school…"

"I'm just saying, if you wanted to."

Rowan squinted like he was thinking about something, but he was quick to clear it away. "Okay," he whispered.

"Do you want to start using condoms?" I asked.

His test results crinkled under my grip, and I smoothed them out again with steady fingers, waiting for his reply.

"I don't know, Gil," he finally answered, eyes downcast. "I'm not just new to men, I'm new to all of this."

It had been far too easy to forget that Rowan hadn't been with a man before me. That he hadn't warned me or even hinted that I was about to be his first. He'd been so eager and awkward, I thought he was just nervous, and I'd spread him out and fucked him like he had twenty years of practice taking a cock up his ass.

Sighing, I tossed his test results onto my coffee table.

"How about we keep things as they are for now, but when you decide to start dating someone else, we start using condoms," I suggested, forcing out the next sentence like the words were wrapped with barbs. "Or stop the whole thing entirely."

"I don't want to stop."

It was a relief in some ways. A burden in others.

"That's fine for now," I agreed.

"Good. Great." Rowan straightened his posture and smiled at me. "That's settled."

"It's settled," I said, completely smitten with every

single thing about him. "You should go pick up that pizza. I'm sure Fisher's hungry and waiting for you."

"What?" he asked, brows knit in confusion.

"Your son," I reminded. "You were just stopping by here on your way to get him dinner."

"Oh! Yeah. Right."

Rowan turned quickly for my front door, muttering something under his breath I couldn't quite make sense of.

"I'll see you soon, Rowan," I promised once he stepped onto my porch.

"When?"

I wanted to tell him *whenever you want*, but carte blanche didn't feel very casual to me. Carte blanche felt very close to intimate.

"Can you come over Friday night? After Fisher is asleep?"

"We used to watch movies on Friday nights," Rowan said, bobbling his head side to side. "I'm trying to start it up again."

"That's why I said after he's asleep."

"It'll be late."

Late was casual.

Late was perfect.

"I know," I said.

"Maybe you can come over after the movie is finished instead?" he proposed.

"You're too loud," I told him.

Rowan pulled his lips between his teeth, pupils dilating into dark, black pools.

"Another time," I conceded. "Come over Friday night, however late it is."

"Okay," he rasped, not making any move to leave.

"Go get your pizza, Rowan."

He barked out a hoarse laugh, stepping backward and off my porch. He managed to catch himself before falling, adjusting his bowtie and smoothing his hands down the front of his shirt before turning and heading down to where he'd parked his car. I watched him go, wondering all the while if I wanted to tell him that his son already suspected there was something going on between us.

Fisher had all but implied it Saturday morning when he'd shown up uninvited. I hadn't confirmed or denied, and I didn't know anything about having kids, but I knew they were terrifyingly smart and attentive. The less time I spent at Rowan and Fisher's place, the better, because another thing I knew about kids was they were impressionable, and the last thing I wanted was for Fisher to get the impression that I was around for anything more than a good time with his father.

Rowan and I were good in bed. Hell, we were great in bed, but that was where our compatibility started and ended. He was too proper, too maintained, too talkative for me. And he had Fisher which, as great of a kid as he seemed to be, was still a deal breaker for me.

"It doesn't matter," I told myself, locking the door and walking into the kitchen. I turned the lights on as I went. A reminder of how holed up in my office I'd been for the whole day. The kitchen lights were glaringly white, but they made it very clear I didn't have anything worth eating in my fridge. Nothing more than a six-pack of beer with one bottle left inside. I cursed under my breath and slammed the fridge closed.

Pizza sounded perfect, but there was no way I was going to head into town after Rowan and meet up with him on accident in the takeout line. My options were sandwiches, Chinese, or I could take a ride to Ridgecrest and get a pizza there. I passed the crumpled test results on my coffee table, my fingers itching to check them one more time and I knew staying local wasn't an option.

I needed to get on my bike and get out of town before I did something stupid and forgot what the word *casual* fucking meant.

CHAPTER 15
ROWAN

Maybe now that we'd agreed we weren't anything, I'd stop being so painfully clumsy around Gil. It wasn't like I'd hoped for a relationship, or wanted one, but knowing there was no possibility of us evolving into something more than neighbors who fucked sometimes should have taken the pressure off.

And it might have if I could've made myself stop thinking about him for more than three minutes at a time. Replacing the bathroom floor took twice as long as it should have because my mind kept wandering to Gil and how easy it was to be around him. Even when I was falling over myself and fumbling the conversation. A patient kind of understanding radiated off him, almost like he didn't mind what a bumbling dolt I could be at times.

I burned dinner last night thinking about Gil and those test results he'd shoved in my mailbox. Neither one of us had been the most responsible at the start, but it lit a fire low in my belly to know that he'd thought about me when I wasn't around.

Thinking about him while I was at work was the most dangerous, though Because I could ill afford for my new colleagues to see the effect it had on me. And I liked the people at me new office. It wasn't that I didn't like my old colleagues, but I'd always held myself apart from them for one reason or another.

Eric had often accused me of using Fisher as a reason to not have my own life. He hadn't even stopped when I explained that Fisher was my life. He'd looked so fucking sad that I almost wanted to punch him.

And what about when he's all grown up, Rowan? What then?

The asshole had a point. Hell, Fisher was half grown now. Twelve going on twenty. Biking to and from school every day on a bike that he could suddenly fix himself. Part of it was the help he'd gotten from Gil, and part of it was likely all the videos he'd been watching on bike repair. The point was that Fisher didn't need me as much as he used to and Eric had been right. I needed a life outside of Fisher.

"Excuse me," a voice caught me off-guard and my attention snapped away from my computer screen, which I'd spent the past five minutes staring at without seeing a damn thing. I turned to the doorway of my office and furrowed my brow in confusion. I didn't have any clients scheduled for the next hour.

"Hi, can I help you?"

The man walked into my office and extended his hand. "Brian Wallace. I work in the next office over. We sometimes borrow your photocopier when ours is on the fritz, which is always. I just wanted to stop in and introduce myself."

Brian was a bean pole of a man. All lanky limbs that he managed to maneuver with more grace than I ever could. His dark hair was artfully shaggy, the kind of look that I knew took more effort than not. Dark brown eyes sparkled at me when I shook his hand.

"Rowan Verne. I'm new here, obviously."

Brian had a folder clutched in his other hand and my gaze drifted to it. "Did you need the copier, or have you already been?" I pulled my hand away and resisted the urge to wipe it on the side of my pants. I might not always have the best gay-dar on the planet, but when someone looked at me like I was an actual snack, it was impossible to miss.

"Oh, I've already been, but thanks." Brian's gaze slid away from me. "You have a kid? How old?"

I turned my attention to the direction Brian had been looking. He'd spotted the picture of Fisher on my desk, and anyone with eyes could tell that he was mine. "Twelve."

"Mine too. Twelve going on fifty." Something in Brian softened when he talked about his kid. "Jackson grew up awful fast when his dad and I divorced." Brian shook his head and met my gaze with a sheepish one. "I didn't mean to get all personal like that. I really did come to introduce myself."

"It's fine. I'm the king of awkward." Being around Brian was easier than being around Gil for that exact reason. Around Gil I was forever flustered. Tripping over my feet and my tongue. And Gil hadn't minded. He hadn't minded so much that he'd left his test results in my mailbox and had promised to see me again. Tonight.

"Look, I'm going to put myself out of my misery and confess that I'd spotted this cute redhead who was new to town and I wanted to introduce myself, so I made up a story." Brian flipped the folder open to reveal it was empty. "I'd love it if we could do lunch sometime."

"Lunch would be fine. I'd like that."

"Did I say lunch? I meant dinner. Maybe tonight?"

Thoughts of Gil flashed again into my head. And the truth smacked me in the face. I didn't want to say yes to a date with Brian because I'd have to tell Gil. And I didn't want to tell Gil because I desperately needed to know what it was like to have all of him. I was greedy and needy when it came to him. I wanted to bask in his intensity and wallow in his attention. He made me feel like prey that had been caught, rolling over in surrender. Showing him my soft underbelly.

"Ah… maybe lunch?"

Brian's smile didn't falter. "I knew I was pushing my luck, but you can't blame a guy for trying. Are you free for lunch one day next week?"

Lunch I could do. Lunch during the week was hardly a date.

"I could do lunch. I'm usually free."

"Then it's a date."

"It's lunch," I clarified, not wanting to give him the wrong idea.

Brian's smile fell a little, but he forced it back to its full brightness. "It's lunch, then. See you around, Rowan."

Brian had no sooner left and I'd slumped into my office chair when Morgan appeared.

"What did Brian want?" Morgan asked as if he already knew exactly what went down and just wanted me to confirm it for him.

"To ask me to lunch." I left out the part about him trying to get a dinner date out of me instead.

"Makes sense. You're pretty much his exact type."

"He's got a thing for redheads?"

"He's got a thing for single men." Morgan seemed to know more about Brian, but instead of spilling it, he clammed up, tucking his knowledge away like a secret treasure. "What did you say?"

"I said yes to lunch, no to dinner."

"He's a good guy, Rowan. If you were looking for someone to vouch for him."

"I really wasn't. But dinner after a two second conversation is a little fast for me." I ignored the fact that I'd fucked Gil without knowing him at all. Without a date. Without a nice safe get-to-know-you period. There was something magnetic about him that I couldn't stay away from and was powerless to resist.

"My apologies." Morgan didn't look all that upset that I wasn't going to go out with Brian. At least not yet. I might take him up on that dinner invitation eventually. Maybe on a night when I wasn't itching to see Gil again.

"I did agree to lunch with him next week. But just as friends. Or people who intend to be friends. If you know him so well, you should come with us." It would feel less like a date that way, but I didn't want to tell Morgan that.

"I'll see what my schedule is like."

I wasn't sure if he was being serious, or just using it as an excuse to say no later as opposed to saying no right now. Not that it mattered. I still had a meeting to get through. And then I had to hit the grocery store, the hardware store, and the Thai place on the way home.

Morgan slipped out of my office without a word and I threw myself into my work. Burying thoughts of Gil and Brian and whatever matchmaker bullshit Morgan had been up to, I got through the rest of my day without making an ass of myself and with minimal mind-wandering.

It was like there was a countdown clock in my brain ticking the seconds away until I got to see Gil again. It had been there since the last time I saw him and shamelessly pursued him, and agreeing to his terms had been the easy part. I had a terrible feeling there wasn't a whole lot I wouldn't do to see him again.

The thing about being single for so long was that I'd forgotten how nice it was to be touched by hands that weren't mine. And Gil had amazing hands. Strong. Capable. Rough when they needed to be. Gentle when it wasn't expected sometimes. Just like him.

I arrived home to find Fisher slumped on the couch, his earbuds in, scrolling through his phone. He raised his head and glanced at me and the pizza I carried, balanced with one hand while I hauled in the bags of groceries with the other.

"There's another bag or two in the car. Can you go get them?"

Fisher let out a sigh, but got to his feet and shuffled out the door without shoes on. It reminded me of when he was little and refused to wear shoes for months. The only thing that got him back into shoes were the kind that lit up when you walked.

Fisher came into the kitchen and set the bags on the floor before he started rummaging around in them.

"You know you could put some of those away, right?"

He rolled his eyes, but began putting things where they belonged.

"How was school?"

"Fine."

I eyed him for a moment, until he noticed me staring and, in true almost-teenager fashion, scoffed at me. "It was fine, Dad."

"I was just wondering." I tried to act more nonchalant than I felt, but the truth was I was waiting for the other shoe to drop. Waiting for Fisher to come home and shrink into himself even more than usual. I was waiting to find out that moving here had been a huge mistake and that he was more miserable than ever.

"Trust me, Dad. If this place sucked, I'd let you know." He shoved the canned goods onto a shelf with no regard for what way the labels faced or whether they were in neat rows or with similar products.

But I didn't care about that. Fisher's comment was high praise coming from his twelve year-old mouth. He'd been apathetic about the move, but maybe that was because he didn't want to get his hopes up that this would be a better place. Hearing that it didn't suck was a few steps away from hearing that he was happy here. It meant that he could be happy here, that he saw the potential.

Or maybe he was twelve and he meant that it didn't

suck and I was reading far too much into things the way I tended to do. The way I tried desperately not to about a certain neighbor and a late-night date. Only it wasn't a date. Gil made that clear. It was just sex. Sex until I started dating someone who wanted to date me. I could live with that arrangement.

CHAPTER 16
GIL

'd spent more time that week thinking about Rowan than I should have. Especially considering he wasn't meant to be anything more than a casual fuck. I'd gone for a ride every night to try and clear him out of my head, but nothing had worked. As soon as the bike hit eighty, I so easily imagined him on the back with his arms wrapped tight around my stomach, his chest pressed against my back. When I'd come to a stop, the fantasy was always quick to evaporate. Rowan wasn't the kind of man to climb onto the back of a 1000cc motorcycle. He wasn't even the type to know what that meant.

So when Friday night rolled around, I tried to not pace my living room as the clock ticked on past eight, past nine, past ten. It was seven minutes after eleven when Rowan finally showed up at my door, face flushed and chest heaving.

"Did you walk here?" I asked, stepping to the side to let him in.

He nodded.

When he brushed past me, I could smell his soap, a hint of pizza sauce on his fingers, and I was feral. Pushing the door closed behind him, I cornered him in against the wall and wasted no time before crashing our mouths together. Rowan made a surprised sound into my mouth that I was quick to swallow, even quicker to slide my hands down to the backs of his thighs to heft him up off the ground. He wrapped his legs around my waist, his arms around my neck, and he let me devour him whole right there against my front door.

"Good to see you too," he murmured against my mouth.

I turned us away from the door and dropped him unceremoniously onto my couch. I hadn't planned on getting far with him, so during one of my many circles around the house while waiting, I'd brought a bottle of lube to the coffee table so I could be ready for any scenario. I'd never loved myself more than in that moment.

Breaking away from Rowan's mouth, I kissed my way down the side of his neck, using my body to grind against him in a hard and teasing kind of slide. He dug his fingernails into the small of my back, gasping and moaning and arching into me like he'd been hungry for my dick his entire life and not just the past few weeks.

"You look indecent in these sweats," I whispered against his ear, reaching between us and fighting the gray sweats from our last encounter down his legs and eventually off. Folding myself back on top of him, I bent one of Rowan's knees back toward his shoulder, the other sprawled out off the side of the couch.

"They're just gray sweats," he said.

I stretched past him for the lube, doing everything I could to ignore just how painfully aroused Rowan made me. How had I gone two years not caring about sex at all, being fine with jerking off every couple of days and coming into the shower drain? I couldn't reconcile that man with the version of myself who was achingly hungry for this red-haired stranger, the one who needed his body so desperately. I was torn between wanting to pump load after load of cum inside of him and coming across his hip in a wild spray, then using my finger to trace my spend between the constellation of his freckles.

I wanted both.

I would have both.

"You're wearing too many clothes," he complained, fingers fighting against the waistband of my black joggers.

"Be patient, Row. I'll let you have my cock as many times as you need it tonight."

He cursed under his breath and I slid two slick fingers between the cheeks of his ass. Teasing his hole with one, I pressed softly against his rim with the other.

"Bear down," I whispered to him. "Let me in. Show me how much you want me."

He did, and my finger slipped inside of him with hardly any resistance. I twisted around and pressed against his prostate, which earned me a surprised gasp and a violent flush across his cheeks. I kissed his freckles and added a second finger, then a third. By the time he was prepped for me, Rowan was a sweaty and writhing mess on my couch, his shirt rucked up beneath his chin and his cock violently hard and wet against his stomach.

I was just as hard, if not more, and I had to take a

handful of steadying breaths when I pushed down on my shaft to notch the head of my dick against his hole. He was still folded in half for me, spread open and desperate. He was going to make someone really fucking happy someday, but for now, all he had to work with was me.

"Do it again, baby," I coaxed, rolling my head back to look at the ceiling instead of the man laid out beneath me. "Let me come in that tight hole of yours."

It wasn't the first time I'd taken him bare. In fact, we'd been careless every time before this one, but it *was* the first time I knew I could finish inside of him. It was a small change on paper, but massive enough in my head that I almost ended the night as soon as the swollen crown of my cock popped past that tight muscle. Groaning, I bracketed my hands around his slender hips and steadied myself.

There was barely any of my cock inside of him, and Rowan whimpered, fingers scrabbling at my wrist.

"Please, more," he begged, bearing down around me again.

"I know what you need, Rowan," I whispered, feeding him another inch of my shaft, then another. "It's coming."

Before long, I was fully seated inside of him, our bodies pressed together in all of the best places and ways. Rowan blinked up at me like I was a miracle, throat bobbing with every breath and swallow.

Suddenly, it didn't feel very casual anymore.

I fell forward, covering his eyes with my palm. I couldn't bear to see the way he looked up at me. It was too much and undeserved.

"Gil," he protested, but didn't fight me off. He curled one hand around my wrist, almost in question.

"I'm going to fucking defile you," I promised him. "Going to do the dirtiest fucking things to this body of yours, and I don't want you to see it. Don't want to ruin you with it."

Didn't want to ruin him with me, but that was a difference that didn't matter.

He flexed his fingers around my wrist before letting them fall away, and it was all the consent I needed. Drawing my hips back, I slammed forward into Rowan again so hard the feet of the couch skittered against the wood floors. He cried out, but quickly snapped his mouth closed, pulling his lips between his teeth.

"You can be loud here," I reminded him. "There's no one to hear you scream but the man who's making you."

I slammed into him a second time, a third, a fourth, until he received my message and let himself go. Rowan thrashed, spreading his legs wider, begging and pleading for me to fuck him harder, to fuck him deeper. I couldn't get the leverage I needed with my hand on his face, but I didn't trust myself to look into his eyes either.

Pulling out before I made another bad decision, I hauled Rowan to his feet and turned him toward the hallway.

"Bedroom," I demanded. "I want to take you from behind."

He practically ran to my room, climbing onto my bed and arranging himself on his hands and knees. The sight of him was indecent, with his lube-slicked ass on display, his cock and balls heavy between his legs.

"Can I spank you?" I asked, finally getting all the way out of my pants and climbing onto the bed behind him.

"I've never—"

"That wasn't what I asked."

Rowan buried his face into my pillow. "Yes."

I spanked his ass once, hard enough to leave a welt shaped like my hand. He cried out and arched his back, begging once again to be filled. I obliged him, sinking back home in one smooth stroke. It was easier to fuck Rowan like this, without his gorgeous blue eyes blinking up at me, drunk with lust and some other feelings he had no right sharing with me. I didn't know what my face would say in return, so it was better to stay behind him, to focus on the curve of his hips, the knobs of his spine, the plump globes of his ass.

Rowan took my cock like he was born to do it, making it easy to forget that, until me, he'd never been with a man before. Toys were nothing compared to the real thing, I knew, and I tried to slow my pace to something less punishing.

"What's wrong?" Rowan asked, turning his head to the side.

I pushed his face into the pillow, his body into the tangled mess of my sheets. "I don't want to hurt you."

"You're not," he said.

"Not yet."

"I'm not breakable."

It was the bravest and boldest thing he'd ever said to me. Maybe the first thing he'd ever said that didn't come with an uncertainty or a stutter. Rowan was clearly comfortable on his knees for me with my cock inside of him, my handprint on his ass. There was no reason for me to go easy on him because of my own worries, which were clearly not warranted or welcome.

"Okay," I whispered.

Digging my fingers into the swell of his ass, I pulled him apart so I could get a better view of the way his body took me inside.

"You're swallowing my cock whole," I said softly, tracing one of my fingers around the place where our bodies were joined. He shivered, and a bead of sweat rolled down my temple. "You feel so fucking good, Rowan. I want you to come on my cock. I want you to fucking come for me."

His hand disappeared beneath him, and his breathy moans turned to low growls. I fucked into him with the same rhythm he fucked himself, his muscles clenching and grabbing at me in all new kinds of ways as he tried to bring himself off.

"Don't stop talking," he choked out, a tremor rolling through his entire body.

I huffed, dick pulsing inside of him.

"Do you like when I talk dirty to you, Row? Do you like when I talk you through it?"

"Yes."

I growled, snapping my hips hard and chasing after every possible inch of depth I could find.

"I can't wait to come in this gorgeous asshole of yours," I told him, and it was the truth. "I want to put so much cum inside of you that it spills out and makes a mess of you. I'll lick it up, baby. Push it back inside of you with my tongue, put some of it into your mouth so you can taste the way you make me feel. Would you li—"

Rowan's body went tense and he screamed.

He actually fucking screamed.

It was like the orgasm took control of his body, and he bucked ferociously beneath me, every muscle spasming as he shot his load onto my sheets. He was still deep in the aftershocks of it when I started to move again. My grip around his hips was so punishing I worried it would bruise, but just like with his release, my own need had taken over.

I fucked into Rowan again hard, throwing my head back with a snarl as my orgasm slammed into me like a brick wall. It hurt to come, jet after jet of cum pouring out of my dick and right into his ass. Just like I'd promised. I didn't think it would be enough to spill out of him, but it might have been.

The aftershocks of my orgasm vibrated through me long after my cock stopped spilling, and I collapsed on top of Rowan, turning us both onto our sides so I didn't have to leave him just yet. We stayed on our sides, breathing ragged and loud, not speaking for God knew how long. Eventually, my cock softened and slipped out of him. He winced, and I lowered my hand between us to make good on my earlier promise.

I chased my cum from the back of his balls and his taint, pushing it back inside of him with one slow thrust of my finger. Rowan shuddered and moaned, then fucked himself down onto my hand like he wanted more. I admired his dedication to the cause, but I needed a breather if he wanted another round.

"I can't fuck you again just yet," I said, an apology.

"In a minute." His words were a little slurred, but I closed my eyes and nodded.

"Yeah, Row. In a minute."

CHAPTER 17
ROWAN

I should've gone home the minute Gil softened and slipped out of me. Or in the moments after, when he slid his leaking cum back inside me. Or in the moments after that when we were quiet and content in a way that didn't make sense for two men who weren't anything to each other.

Instead, I stayed. I basked in the closeness of another person. The way his body wrapped around mine even after we'd finished. Maybe I was touch-starved, but it felt almost too good to lie there in the quiet. There was some kind of magic when I was with Gil, some kind of spell he cast on me, because when I was with him, I felt so much like *me* that I almost didn't recognize myself. And Gil never seemed to mind how inept that made me.

Having gotten what I came for, I should have gone home. But when I stirred, Gil tightened his hold on me like his body didn't want me to go, even if he couldn't make his mouth ask me to stay.

Rolling over, I faced him and he gave me a sleepy

smile without meeting my gaze. His focus was on my mouth, so I gave it to him. I leaned in and kissed him. The kiss we shared when I arrived had been all hunger and anticipation coming to fruition. Now, it was lazy and slow. Satisfied, but still needy. It fed my appetite, making me hard again. As my pulse started to race, I felt the throb of Gil's handprint on my ass. If I hadn't been so shocked that I liked it so much, I probably would have shot my load right then.

Coming over to Gil's house felt like the most reckless thing I'd done, maybe ever. But I couldn't stop myself even if I wanted to. Kissing my way down his body, he easily let me roll him onto his back. I settled myself between his legs and dragged my lips over the sensitive skin at the inside of his thigh. The light dusting of dark hair was impossibly soft. A stark contrast to the rock solid cock that lay against his stomach.

I dragged my gaze up his body, taking in the flat planes of his abdomen, his only slightly furry chest. The intensity in his eyes had me looking away, burying my face in the short thatch of hair around his cock.

"Gil." I swallowed around my desire. "Talk me through it."

There was something comforting about the way he'd talked when he fucked me. I liked that he never gave me a chance to think or question if I was doing things right. He took over and looked after us both, and I wanted that again. The peace that came with knowing I was what he wanted.

At least in the moment.

A shiver travelled down my body from the place where Gil's fingers slid into my hair, all the way down to the tips of my toes. They curled when he tightened his grip. "Open your mouth for me, Row."

I dug my hands into his sides and did as I was told. Part of me thought he might unceremoniously rammed his dick in my mouth, but I should have thought better. Because Gil didn't. Of course he didn't. Instead he angled his cock and brushed it over my parted lips. My tongue darted out to lick him, earning me a rumble in the back of his throat that went straight to my balls.

"Is this what you need?" Gil asked as he dragged his cock back and forth.

"Gil, please." My cock already ached and my hole clenched when I thought of taking him again. I could still feel him there. Feel him in me. The press of his finger as he'd tucked his cum back in my hole like he promised. But it wasn't enough. I wanted to feel him everywhere.

"Go slow, baby. Don't choke." Gil paused as I swirled the tip of my tongue around the head of his cock. "At least not until I tell you to."

God, I needed some friction on my cock. Gil's voice did something to me. Low and raspy, it burrowed into me, under my skin. I could lie here all night and do nothing but listen to him speak filthy words into existence.

But his cock was in my mouth. Hot and hard and slick with my spit as I worked my way down the shaft. Letting my hands wander, I slid one up his chest, brushing my fingers over his nipple. I heard his sharp inhale, then a quiet laugh and Gil pressed down on the back of my head.

"You can take it deeper, can't you, Row? That's right. That's good."

I'd never have been able to say half the things Gil said to me as he cradled my head in both his hands now. He planted his feet on the mattress so he could thrust up into my mouth. And the whole time, he kept talking to me. Kept calling me baby in that rough, sexy voice of his. Kept saying increasingly dirty things until every muscle in my body screamed for release.

He had me aching for him. Throbbing. He'd taken my existence and narrowed it down so it only included him.

"You can take it all, can't you?" Gil gently pressed me down further until my nose was nearly against his skin. When I choked, he let me up. My face felt like I'd stuck it in a volcano it was so hot. Tears sprang to my eyes and I pressed them shut, hoping Gil didn't see the mess I was.

Then his thumbs brushed the tears off my cheeks. "Row, you did so good. You're so good, baby. I need your mouth again."

Gil eased his cock back into my mouth. His breaths rasped in and out of him. The tension in his muscles made his body vibrate.

"I'm going to come in your mouth and I want you to swallow it all, Row."

As if I'd have it any other way.

"Deep breath, that's it. Relax for me." His hips moved faster, but he kept his thrusts shallow, being careful not to gag me again. Though part of me wanted him to, I wanted him to come a whole lot more.

When Gil shattered, I shattered with him. Overcome with the sensation of him unloading in my mouth, of his hands gripping my hair, of the way his legs bracketed me, squeezing slightly when his ass lifted off the bed when he came, I reached between my legs and brought myself off with a couple quick strokes.

I pulled myself off Gil's cock and sucked in a breath. Resting my forehead against his stomach, I was aware of the way Gil very briefly stroked his hands through my hair.

Twice spent. Twice I'd been filled with him and still I wasn't ready to go home.

"I hope you were serious when you said I could have your cock as many times as I needed it tonight, because I don't think I'm done yet." I sat up and met Gil's gaze before bringing my hand to my mouth and cleaning my cum off my fingers.

"Get up here." He reached for me as he spoke, capturing me and yanking me down before flipping me over onto my back. He kissed me hard and deep, his tongue invading my mouth with purpose. "You taste amazing."

Gil blanketed me with his body, warm and soft and perfect.

I didn't mean to fall asleep.

That was my next conscious thought after, *oh fuck*, and, *what time is it?*

Gil was long gone from his bed, the other side cold, but the blankets rumpled. A dent in his pillow where his head had been. I got to my feet and dressed in my clothes that had mysteriously appeared folded at the foot of the bed. I had to get home to Fisher, hopefully before he woke up, but I knew I couldn't walk down the street until I splashed some water on my face and took a piss.

I tried not to let myself panic, but my heart was racing and I felt like a frightened rabbit. Or like a teenager trying to sneak back in before his parents discovered what he'd been up to.

I made quick use of Gil's bathroom to empty my bladder, wash my hands and face, and tidy my hair, in that order. I still looked freshly fucked, but that could've been the panic talking. Gil wasn't in the kitchen, but I could hear the low rumble of his voice in the attached garage. Even though I was sure I'd overstayed my welcome, I couldn't leave without saying something.

I stepped into the garage and saw him leaning against his workbench. His arms were crossed over his chest, and the white shirt he wore did nothing to hide the swell of his arms and the contours of his muscles.

"Hi, Dad."

My head swiveled and I saw Fisher kneeling on the floor of Gil's garage, fiddling with something on his bike. "I got a flat tire and Gil showed me how to fix it."

"That—" I cleared my throat. "That's very nice of him."

"He said he'd take me on his motorcycle." Fisher looked up at me and the brightness of his smile caught me off-guard. I was used to the sullen Fisher, the one with the earbuds in all the time who managed a few syllables here and there if I pressed him to talk to me.

"I said if it was okay with your dad, that I'd take you on my bike. Slowly. Around the block. Maybe up as far as the school."

Fisher looked at me again. "Can I?"

Could he? I was still focused on trying to decide if he knew I'd been here all night. I felt like I'd fallen asleep and woken up in the Twilight Zone.

"I'll leave the two of you to sort this out. I'm going to

get breakfast." He ran a steady hand through his hair. "Can you lock up when you leave?"

He didn't wait for an answer. I stood there a little dumbstruck as Gil put his helmet on, wheeled his bike out of the garage, and roared away without so much as a goodbye.

It shouldn't have hurt my feelings the way it did. We weren't anything, after all. And Gil had just proved how nothing we were.

"So? Can I?" Fisher asked.

His hands were filthy from working on his bike and he had a smear of dirt across his cheek. And he was smiling.

When I didn't answer right away, Fisher tried again, "Gil said he has a spare helmet I can wear. Can I?"

My brain wasn't ready for the idea of my kid on the back of a motorcycle and if it were anyone but Gil, I might have said no. But Fisher hadn't looked so happy in… maybe ever. At least not since well before the move. Gil might be done with me, and maybe it wasn't fair to let my kid get attached, but Fisher looked so excited that I couldn't bring myself to say no.

"I…guess it would be fine."

"Yes!" He dropped the wrench he'd been using and launched himself at me, slinging his arms around me in a hug that was all too welcome, but far too brief. It felt like no time had passed before he pulled away and went back to fixing his bike tire.

"Are you and Gil boyfriends?" Fisher asked with zero regard for my sanity.

"I don't know what we are." I promised myself that

I'd always be honest with my kid. "If we were boyfriends, you'd be okay with that?"

Fisher shrugged. "Gil's cool." He paused what he was doing and glanced up at me. "You smile more now."

My heart lurched at the knowledge that Gil had the same effect on the both of us. But he didn't want anything more than what we'd agreed to and I didn't know how to break that news to Fisher.

Or to myself for that matter, because I sure as hell did want what I wasn't allowed to have.

CHAPTER 18
GIL

I had one bite of donut left when Jack pulled into the parking lot. He drove up alongside the spot my bike was parked in and unrolled the passenger side window down to leer at me.

"Fancy running into you here?" I asked, shoving said last bite into my mouth.

"Any other day, sure." He slid his sunglasses down his nose. "But I knew exactly where to find you today because your boyfriend and step-son pointed me in the right direction."

"He's not…they're not…" I glared at him.

"Get in the fucking car, Valentine. We need to talk."

After plucking the keys out of the ignition of my bike, I sank down into the passenger seat of Jack's car with a groan.

"Rowan spent the night on accident," I explained. "Fisher came over for help with his bike and Rowan walked out."

"How does someone spend the night *on accident?*"

"Well, sometimes, when two people don't care about each other very much at all, they have really exhausting fucking sex and then fall asleep."

Jack sucked his tongue across the front of his teeth and turned his car into an empty parking spot at the other end of the lot. He cut the ignition and reclined the seat all the way. I angled my back against the passenger door and glared down at him.

"Did you come all the way here to harass me about my sex life?" I asked. My fingers were still sticky from the donut...from the sex. "I swear you were just on my ass about not having one, and yet..."

"I absolutely am not here to harass you about developing feelings for a man who has the exact red flag that drove you and my brother apart." Jack folded his hands together behind his head and sighed. "Though it is ironic."

"Rowan and I are just sleeping together."

"His kid seems fond of you."

"I just help him with his bike sometimes."

Jack made an indecipherable noise in the back of his throat and I blew out an exasperated breath. "What did we need to talk about, Jack?"

"My brother."

Dropping my head against the back of the seat, I rubbed the bridge of my nose between my thumb and first finger. The grimace on my face at the mere mention of Philip was enough to have my scar aching like it used to do when it was fresh. I pressed gently against the jagged bottom edge of it, right below my cheekbone, and waited for the pressure to abate.

"What about him?"

"You know I try to keep him out of our relationship."

"I know," I said.

"He's getting married."

"You told me."

Jack scrubbed a hand down his face. "I don't even know how to say this to you."

"Words help," I said simply.

Jack knew me well enough by now to know I wasn't one of those guys who needed grand gestures or declarations. I was a simple man and I appreciated simple communication. It was something Philip, who preferred to beat around the bush instead of facing things head on, never understood. I appreciated, in the present, that Rowan had a good enough head on his shoulders that we'd been able to have the talk we had the night before, to trust we were on the same page about whatever the thing between us was.

Even though I hadn't been scared when I woke up to sunlight streaming through the blinds and his body still soft and warm in my bed. Even though it was the sound of his kid banging again on my door for help with his bike that had woken me up far too early on a Saturday morning. Even though I left them both alone in my garage to discuss whatever the two of them needed to discuss after Rowan had strolled right in on us wearing the same clothes he'd undoubtedly had on for dinner the night before.

Maybe it had been fucked up of me to leave Rowan on his own for that conversation, but I meant what I'd said to him and to Jack. I was not looking to be a boyfriend, least of all a step-parent. Whatever Rowan needed to tell his pre-teen about what he and I did behind closed doors was between the two of them and the two of them alone. I wanted no part in it.

"He's asked me to be his best man," Jack said.

"You told me."

We were not, in fact, covering any new territory with this conversation. He'd already told me Philip was engaged and that he'd been asked to be best man. There had to be something else, but Jack was definitely taking his sweet time getting to it. A loud peal of laughter outside caught my attention and I frowned at the young kid who was running far too close to my bike for comfort. Her parents were distracted, and I wanted to yell at them how dangerous motorcycles were, even when they weren't running. My bike weighed hundreds of pounds and would have easily flattened that toddler into a pancake.

Which begged the question…why had I agreed to take Fisher for a ride?

"It's…" Jack groaned. "They're all coming down pretty hard on me."

"Why? Did you tell him no?"

"My parents are…the way they are," he said.

"I remember."

Their oldest son bringing a man home had been a huge deal for them. For all of us, really. I didn't know at the time that Philip had never even hinted at his bisexuality to his parents—or his brother, for that matter. So, there I was, young and dumb, and walking on sunshine because I thought Philip hung the fucking moon. And I'd found myself on a battlefield filled with hateful glares and vile accusations.

I'd held Philip later that night while he cried about

the whole thing, and I often wondered if it was the pressure from his parents to give them grandchildren that had made the "no kids" thing such a line in the sand for him. Philip and Jack's parents were old-fashioned on a good day, and when I said old-fashioned, I meant racist and homophobic. There was no way around it.

They had learned to tolerate me over time, but…

After Philip and I broke up, all of that initial hate was dumped solely on me. They implied that I'd tricked Philip into being gay, into living in sin. Whatever their issues with him, they all became issues with me. I figured that was easier for all of them so I let it slide off my back as best I could. When Jack resurfaced in my life, to spite all of their words and opinions of me, it had truly meant the world. He never rubbed our continued friendship in his parents' face, and while I knew they thought less of him for it, I imagined they let it slide since there was no risk of me ruining their youngest son's future the way I'd almost done with Philip.

"No one thinks it's right for me to stand up for Philip if you and I are friends," he said softly.

"No one being whom?"

"My parents," he answered. "My brother."

"His fiancé?"

"His future wife."

I couldn't help but laugh at that. Of course he'd gone and found himself a nice girl to marry.

"Where did they meet?" I asked. It didn't matter, but I wanted to know.

"My parents set them up."

"Church?"

"Yes," he answered.

I hummed thoughtfully in the back of my throat, hoping it would vibrate the donut right back into my stomach so I didn't throw up all over Jack's pretty leather dash.

"Is it an ultimatum then?" I asked.

"Yes."

"And what of it, Jack?"

"He's a prick, Gil, but—"

"Right." I didn't need him to say the rest of it. I didn't think I had it in me to hear the words. I grabbed the door handle and shouldered my way out of his car. Jack was quick to raise the seat up, reaching for me over the center console but my legs were too long and I was too fast.

"He's your brother," I finished the sentiment for him, slamming the door closed and bending down so I could see him through the window.

"It's not that simple."

"Ultimatums generally are, Jack." I straightened up and slapped my hand twice against the door. "Thanks for the talk."

I went back to my bike and made quick work of my helmet and the ignition, so even if Jack did call after me, I wouldn't be able to hear him. The last thing I wanted were excuses from the second man in the Sydney family who'd managed to hold my heart in some capacity and break it.

I was stupid.

I should have known better.

My friendship with Jack had always stood on shaky ground after my breakup, and somewhere in the back of my mind, I'd always known it. It had been a good two year run, and I'd just forgotten, that was all. I'd forgotten and I'd let my guard down, and I was doing the exact same thing with Rowan and his annoyingly endearing gap-toothed kid.

Flipping down the visor on my helmet, I sped out of the parking lot, heading up the winding mountain roads far faster than I had any right going. It had been a very long time since I'd ever taken my bike over eighty, but as I hit the midpoint straightaway and I opened her up to one hundred, I had no clue why I'd ever stopped. The wind whipped against my throat, up and off my arms as I raced down the highway. My muscles hurt from the tension it took to stay on the bike at those speeds.

I downshifted quickly as the road sloped into another turn, dropping back to sixty as I finished the ride up the mountain. I'd reached the summit in record time, and since it was still relatively early on a Saturday, the parking lot was mostly deserted. A couple sunrise hikers no doubt had been on the trails for hours, but other than that…

Blessed silence.

I parked on the edge of the lot and yanked off my helmet. My scar ached far more than normal, and when I reached up to massage the tight skin, I found my lash line and my cheek damp. Cursing under my breath, I balanced my helmet on the gas tank and stalked toward the edge of the cliffside. I was by no means suicidal, but being so close to taking myself over was as exhilarating as the speed on the ride up had been.

I'd just lost the most important person in my life, and I had nothing else left to show for it. Life was funny that way. Before Rowan, before Jack, before Philip, I'd been happy with the things that were mine, with the decisions

I'd made. But I was losing these people one by one, and the holes they left were far too massive to fill with other people or with other things.

"Think harder," I said to myself, resting my forehead in my shaking hands. Philip, whom I'd once loved beyond reason was gone. His brother, my best—my only—friend, was on his way out. And Rowan…Rowan shouldn't have even been there in the first place. He'd been dropped into my life unceremoniously and uninvited, but now that he was there…he'd already dug himself a hole too big for anyone else to ever fill.

It was careless of me, maybe, to have been so insistent about things between us staying casual. It was a self-defense mechanism that had already backfired. There was no denying that Rowan stoked a flame inside of me that I never even knew had been lit. When he flushed so red with embarrassment, when he found the strength to be bold and brave.

Everything about him turned me on, made me feel alive.

But some things were still indisputable. I didn't want a relationship and I sure as shit didn't want to be a stepparent.

CHAPTER 19
ROWAN

It was clear that Fisher was enamored with Gil. Maybe obsessed, because suddenly my twelve year-old wanted his own tools and his own side of the garage to work on his bike. The worst of it was that I could hardly blame him since, from the moment I laid eyes on Gil, I'd felt a pull toward him too. A need to know him.

He might as well have kicked me in the stomach when he'd dismissed himself from his own garage the other day. And then running into his friend had been awkward. Jack looked at me and Fisher like we were aliens and our presence in Gil's life was the most astounding thing he'd ever seen. There wasn't a word for how uncomfortable I'd been.

Thankfully, he didn't stick around to wait for Gil once I told him that he'd gone for breakfast. Jack nodded, said it was nice to see us both, and drove off. The way he looked at me lingered, though. Like I was a puzzle he needed to solve. Like it was so unfathomable for me to be standing in Gil's garage that he had to rush off to interrogate his friend.

If they *were* just friends.

I know Jack said they were. And Gil said they were. But that didn't stop me from wondering if maybe Jack didn't want more with Gil and that's why he kept looking at me like I had two heads.

None of that mattered, though, because I didn't hear from Gil for the rest of the weekend. I spent nearly every waking moment renovating my bathroom and obsessing about Gil. I played every interaction with him over and over in my head. He'd been clear from the start. It was just sex. And yet disappointment made my stomach churn.

It was just sex, but it opened me up to the fact that I didn't want just sex with someone. I wanted more. I wanted dates and something with meaning. I'd never really been the kind of guy who jumped from hookup to hookup. I'd always been geared toward wanting a relationship. Something solid.

Monday morning found me in an appointment with a young couple looking to prequalify for their first mortgage. They were fresh off their honeymoon and had received a nice little nest egg from their family as a wedding gift. They wanted to use it toward their down payment.

Happiness oozed from both of them. The way they looked at each other was so saccharine my teeth ached. It was a relief when I was able to usher them out of my office. As they walked out, Brian from the next office over walked in.

"Just the man I came to see." Brian's face lit up like

he was genuinely happy to see me. "I was going for lunch and thought I'd see if you wanted to join me."

My next appointment wasn't until later in the day and I had plenty of time to prepare for it.

"Sure." Why not? It was just lunch. I'd wanted to start over when I moved, and part of that was making friends. Back home, I'd had Eric, but other than him, my social circle was woefully small. I didn't want to fall into the same patterns as before where I worked, raised Fisher, and did nothing else.

Fall had come to the area and it was the perfect autumn day, straight out of a catalog with clear blue skies, crisp mornings, and a bit of heat in the afternoon.

"It sure is nice here this time of year." Inwardly I winced. The worst part of getting to know someone was the small talk portion until you found something in common to bond over. Or found nothing at all.

"There's worse places to live. Believe me. My uncle was in the Army, and my cousins lived all over the place. They hated it growing up, but they all ended up enlisting. Go figure." Brian led me up the street to a little Lebanese place. "You been here yet?"

"Not yet. My kid has been on a mission to sample every pizza place and burger joint in town."

"You can't go wrong with a good pizza. Dotty's has the best, if you haven't been there yet."

"I'll remember that. Thanks."

With so many people milling about during lunch hour, I found myself on the lookout for a familiar man with a shock of white hair and a scar on his face. It was stupid to be hung up on someone who didn't want me.

Well, he wanted me, but only for one thing.

"You okay?" Brian asked as the line inched closer to the counter.

"Yeah, uh, just wondering what to get. I'll admit my knowledge of Lebanese cuisine is limited. As in, I don't have any."

"I'll order us a couple of wraps. I eat here all the time."

Brian ordered a falafel wrap and a shish tawook wrap. He kept the falafel wrap for himself and gave me the other one.

"It's grilled chicken with lettuce, garlic aioli, and pickles."

"Ooh, you took a big gamble picking something with pickles. What if I was one of those pickle haters?"

"Well, then I guess we couldn't be friends."

Friends.

How easy Brian had offered his friendship to me. Gil had offered his body, but nothing else. And the way he'd just taken off the other morning had felt like him slamming the door in my face.

Sure, I could have gone over to his house at any point and talked about it, but I didn't want to come off as needy and desperate, and literally stupid for agreeing to his terms, but wanting him to reconsider. He'd been perfectly clear what we were to each other and I was the idiot who'd actually gone and liked the guy.

Even when I was tripping all over myself, Gil never seemed to mind it much. More than once I'd made an ass of myself around him, but each time he met me with such patience that it was hard not to fall for the guy.

And I wasn't. Falling for him would be stupid. Falling for him would be asking for trouble. Besides, I was out for lunch with someone else, and I was having a perfectly nice time. When I stopped thinking about a certain someone.

With that in mind, I swallowed my bite of wrap and lobbed a question to Brian.

"Have you lived here long, or are you a transplant like me?" There, a perfectly normal question.

Brian had led us over to a table by the windows and we'd sat down and eaten half our meal without talking. My question seemed to open up a floodgate and it was like Brian had just been waiting for the ice to break because he poured out his life story.

"I've lived here all my life. Grew up playing football when I was pretending to be straight, and blowing the players after I came out." He said it with a smirk, like he was fond of the memories. "Got married. Got divorced. Lost custody of a remarkable cat, but he always did like my ex better than me."

"I'm sorry. That's still tough."

Brian shrugged. "I think my ex needed him more than I did." Talk of his ex seemed to trip him up and I wondered if maybe he wasn't the only one hung up on someone else. "What about you? I mean, obviously you're new in town. What brings you here?"

"My company was offering bonus checks to people willing to transfer to understaffed offices. I took the money, bought a house, and here I am. The house still needs a bunch of work, but it's coming along. Slower now that I'm working."

"I'd offer to help, but I'm all thumbs when it comes to DIY. I can manage to check my own oil and change a light bulb if ladders aren't involved. I make a great eggplant parmesan, though, ask any of my dates." Brian's hint at the fact that he'd previously asked me out didn't go unnoticed. I might not be the most socially adept person in the world, but Brian made his interest obvious.

Of course Brian's comment about the light bulb made me think about Gil and him patiently teaching Fisher how to fix his bike. He seemed like the kind of guy who would climb a ladder for me and it was weird that I wanted that. Moving here was supposed to be a fresh start, but already I'd made a mess of things by falling into bed with a man who didn't want me back the same ways I wanted him. But Brian was here, and he was perfectly nice. And attractive. Sure, my brain didn't turn off when he was around, making me act like a fool, but that was okay. Preferable, even.

"So, do you frequently ask strangers to dinner, or was I special?"

Brian's eyes sparkled with mischief. "Well, you see…" He leaned in and lowered his voice like he was sharing a secret. "I've always had a thing for redheads."

"Morgan says you have a thing for single men," I countered, arching a brow.

His mouth twitched into a knowing kind of frown. "In this instance, let's say I have a thing for single redheads."

It was a deflection, but I wasn't going to argue. Brian was single and he was allowed to pursue anyone he wanted. Even me.

"Okay, what would dinner look like if I said yes? What is there to do around here?"

"Well, we could do what the kids do and go through

the drive-thru, then go up to the vista and fog up the windows."

The idea of that didn't suck, but I could barely picture myself in a fogged-up car with Brian. I was thirty-five, and he was lucky I could picture it at all, but it definitely wasn't him in the seat next to me when I did.

"What do grown-ups do for fun around here?"

"There's bingo every Thursday night at six at the senior center." He grinned at me.

"There's got to be a happy medium between the two."

"Maybe. If I took you out for dinner, I'd pick you up at your house and I'd take you to my favorite restaurant. I'm there all the time, so we'd get a nice quiet table that was a bit out of the way from everyone. And after we ate, I'd take you to the art gallery because you look like an art gallery kind of guy."

"And what does an art gallery kind of guy look like?"

Brian's gaze flicked down to my throat where I'd neatly tied a bowtie that morning.

"Well, I can't say for sure, but I bet they wear bowties. And I bet they're the kind of guy who doesn't like going to a movie on a first date because you can't get to know someone in a dark theater, at least not in the ways you want to know a person. The way I want to know you."

The exact way Gil didn't want to know me.

Maybe I was using Brian. I knew there'd be nothing between us, but I couldn't just sit around at home and hope that Gil would one day decide he wanted me for more than sex. Brian was attractive, but I wasn't attracted to him. My heart didn't skip a beat looking at him. I didn't get so nervous I couldn't function and fell all over myself.

And yet…

"So when would this date happen, if I were to say yes?"

"If you said yes, I'd take you out Wednesday night, with hopes that it went well enough for a repeat on Friday night."

"That's ambitious. But…" I took a deep breath and convinced myself that this was the right thing to do. I wanted something more than midnight hookups. "Wednesday works for me, if it works for you."

Brian's smile was wide and bright and his enthusiasm almost made me back out. He was clearly more invested in the idea than I was, but maybe I'd come around.

I couldn't stay hung up on Gil forever, could I?

CHAPTER 20
GIL

Jack had been trying to call me all week, but I kept sending him to voicemail. I knew it was only a matter of time before he actually showed up at my house, but it was Wednesday and he'd yet to go that far. I hadn't really heard from Rowan, which was fine. Our relationship didn't require daily check-ins, and I knew he had his hands full with Fisher, his job, and all the work that needed to be done on the house.

Another reason I'd never wanted to be a parent was because I never wanted to risk being a single parent. I didn't have the patience for that kind of thing. I barely had the patience for Fisher, but there he was again, like a goddamn barnacle. I set down my beer—the first one of the night—and used the back of my hand to wipe sweat off my forehead as he cruised his bike up my driveway. He shoved down the kickstand with an unhappy sound, setting his bike to rest right beside my motorcycle.

"Do you have any soda?" he asked, glancing at my beer.

"No."

He fidgeted with the earbud in his right ear.

"Are those on?" I asked.

He shook his head.

"Then take them off."

He huffed, but pulled both earbuds out and put them into his pocket. "Can I have that ride on your bike?"

No hello.

No how are you.

"It's almost dinner, isn't your dad expecting you home?"

"He's on a date," Fisher said with a shrug. "He left me money for pizza."

"A date?" My voice cracked on the ask, which was embarrassing, but if Fisher noticed it—which I'm sure he did—he had the decency to not call me out about it.

"With some guy from work. Brian, I think."

The single drink of beer I'd taken roiled around my stomach and I tossed the whole bottle into the trash. Rowan was allowed to date. In fact, I should have been encouraging it. I'd made it very clear to him what I wanted and what I could offer and dating wasn't on the table.

So why did the thought of him being out with another man make my skin crawl?

The thought of another man becoming familiar with the sharp jut of Rowan's hip bone and the cluster of freckles that danced up toward his waist made me want to break Brian-from-work's fucking hand.

"Oh."

"They had lunch on Monday, Dad said," Fisher went

on, unbothered at the storm building in the middle of my chest.

"Cool," I said, feeling very *not* cool about the whole thing.

"He said not to wait up for him."

"Yeah." I slammed down the hood of the Cougar and shot Fisher a scathing look. "Let's go for a ride."

If he was on the bike, he couldn't fucking keep talking. Well, he could talk, but I wouldn't be able to hear him and that was the only blessing I needed.

"Really?"

"Yeah. Move your bike out of the way. I'm gonna go grab you a jacket and helmet from inside."

I slammed the door on my way into the house, needing to shake off some of the energy that had begun to manifest itself in my bones after finding out Rowan was out on a date. I knew Rowan worked at the bank, so that meant Brian worked at the bank, because he'd never be the kind of man to date a customer, and I was relatively confident Brian from the bank didn't know how to make Rowan come as good as I did. So even if their date went that far, it would have to be their last one, right?

That was what I told myself as I got my leather jacket out of the closet. I grabbed a spare for Fisher, even though he'd be swimming in it. Some protection was better than nothing. I dug out a spare helmet from the hall closet, thankful that Fisher was close enough to adult size that it would fit him well.

Back in the garage, I got him zipped up and clipped in. Even with his face pinched behind the pads of the helmet, I could tell he was flushed and excited.

"I want my dad to be happy again," he said, and I

thought about Rowan and Brian before snapping the visor down in place to shut Fisher up for the second time.

"He deserves it," I agreed, wheeling my bike out of the garage so there'd be more room for Fisher to climb onto the back.

After I got him situated and explained all the safety rules to him, I turned the key. The roar of the engine wasn't loud enough to drown out Fisher's excited yelp, and I patted the top of his hands after they tightened around my stomach.

"You ready?" I asked.

He nodded like a big bobblehead behind me.

And we were off.

Rowan had technically only approved a ride to around the block, but he was out on a date which meant Fisher and I had nothing but time, and even with a twelve year-old clamped on behind me, I still did my best thinking on the bike. I rolled to a stop when we reached the end of the street, checking in on Fisher again.

"You good?"

"Oh, my God, this is the best!" he shouted through the helmet.

I chuckled and set off, not going so far as to take him up the mountains on his first ride. Those turns were sharp and steep, and I didn't trust him to stay on the back. Instead, I rode us around the edges of town, deliberately avoiding the main streets where all the restaurants were since the last thing I wanted was to run into Rowan.

That might have been a lie.

I found I wanted to see Rowan far more than I should, but I definitely didn't want to see him on a date. What I wanted to do was go home, call Jack, and try to make sense of the very unexpected feelings that had suddenly come up out of nowhere, but Jack was my ex's brother and he'd picked his side. I was well and truly alone, save for the pre-teen behind me whom I'd lose as soon as Rowan found someone who could give him all of the things he deserved.

Fisher's voice in my head saying how he wanted his dad to be happy was loud as a cannon shot and on repeat as I finally looped the perimeter of town and headed back to my house. Rowan had been a married man; he had a son to raise. Happy for him was a partner and dinner dates and school plays, or whatever kids like Fisher did. Happy for Rowan was not going to be coming over at the end of the night for a quick bang and hoping he didn't fall asleep before sneaking out to go back home.

I was going to lose him.

I was already losing him.

When I rode up my driveway and came to a stop, Fisher was off the bike immediately, yapping and gesturing with his hands. I unclipped the strap at the bottom of his helmet and yanked it up over his head.

"—the wind! That was so cool and you went really fast on Miller Road and I thought I was gonna fly right off, but I didn't."

I'd barely gone forty-five on Miller Road.

I reached out and tugged the pull on the zipper, divesting Fisher of my spare leather jacket.

It had been Philip's once.

"I'm glad you had fun," I told him. "You should probably head home and get that pizza now."

"Ignoring my dad is only fun if he's home," Fisher said, reaching back into his pocket for his earbuds. He popped them in, and I knew he didn't have any music on. I would have to let Rowan know his kid was scamming him half the time. "Can you teach me how to change oil or something?"

I scoffed, rolling my eyes at him. "That's your dad's job."

"He pays someone to change his. I don't think he knows how."

"I'm sure he does."

"Can't you just teach me since we're here?" Fisher pressed.

"I don't need to change any oil." The Cougar hadn't run in over a year. It needed a new engine, not fresh oil.

"What about a tire or something?"

A laugh bubbled out of me, and I waved Fisher off dismissively. "I don't have any tires to change tonight, kid."

"You were out here to do something on it when I showed up."

"I was out here to drink and think," I corrected him.

"The hood was up!" Fisher pointed at the Cougar. "You had a wrench."

"I was *thinking*," I assured him. "What grade are you in? Tenth? They have shop at the school."

"I'm in seventh."

I had no fucking clue about kids.

"It's too late to be working on cars," I said. "But when I'm ready to, I'll let your dad know and you can come over."

I didn't even have Rowan's phone number. I bet Brian did.

"Fine," Fisher grumbled.

His hair was a mess from the helmet, and he still had indents on the sides of his face. He muttered under his breath the whole time he got situated back on his bike, the protests only quieting down once he was out of earshot. I watched him go, then sat in the silence of my garage until the stillness hurt my ears.

I closed the big door and brought all Philip's old gear back inside. Instead of putting it back into the closet where it belonged, I left it sitting on the coffee table. Maybe as a reminder or a punishment, I wasn't sure. I thought about calling him, which was probably the worst idea I'd ever had, second only to taking Rowan Verne to bed more than one time.

The worst part about Philip getting married was that it was the only thing I'd ever wanted for him. I loved Philip and I wanted him to be happy. I wanted his parents to be happy with him, and that wasn't a future he ever could have had with me. He'd risked so much by bringing me home to meet them, just by being with me in the first place. I'd never truly appreciated the sacrifices he'd made for me until we were already split up, but it was those realizations that made me confirm I didn't want to be in a relationship ever again.

The sacrifices were worth it, he'd told me. Jack had said the same thing. That's just what you did when you loved somebody. You sacrificed, and I thought that was the stupidest thing I'd ever heard. I never imagined love to be the kind of thing that required you to shave off parts of yourself to make another person whole, and that was what Philip and I had done for each other. I hoped the woman he was about to marry was whole on her own, without needing to make changes to fit the person

Philip—and his parents—wanted her to be. I hoped Jack could be as good a friend to her as he'd been to me. I hoped…

I hoped all sorts of things all through the rest of the night, and I wish I could say when Rowan showed up on my porch at ten-fifteen in gray chinos, a pink button-up, and a blue and yellow bowtie, that I turned him away. His hair was a little messy, loose curls tangled on the top of his head, and when I opened the door he smelled like the ocean.

He was wearing cologne.

"Hey," I said, swallowing back all the bile that was trying to force its way out of my mouth since Fisher had shown up hours earlier.

"Hey." The corner of his mouth quirked up a little, and I loved how Rowan didn't stutter around me anymore. "Can I come in?"

I looked up him and down, checking his clothes to make sure he was all in order. His hair was the only unkempt thing about him, and all I'd have to do was pull his pants down two inches to find the scattering of freckles I wanted to mark as my own.

Rowan was nothing if not an honest man.

If he'd fucked this Brian guy, he would tell me. More so, I'd be able to tell without him even saying a word. Rowan wore his heart on his sleeve and his emotions on his face. His arrival on my porch confirmed their date had ended early and without any clothes coming off. That should have been a relief, but it was barely more than a band aid on a flesh wound.

My time was running out.

"Yeah," I said, voice low and scratchy. "Come on in."

CHAPTER 21
ROWAN

The date was fine. Fine, except for the fact that everything Brian did, I found myself comparing him to Gil. Fine, except for the fact that even going on a date made my stomach tight and unhappy, like I was doing something bad. Like cheating on Gil. Except Gil and I weren't anything that would restrict me from going on a date. I knew where I stood with him. Going on a date with Brian was *fine*.

A fine fucking mistake. Dinner was awkward, and not in a way that anyone would find endearing. Conversation was hard to come by, though Brian tried his best, to his credit. We went on a walk after and he bought us ice cream. At some point during the ice cream, Brian gave up. With a sigh, he tossed the rest of his ice cream in a trash can and looked at me.

"It's not happening, is it?"

The answer was a resounding no. I managed a meek shake of my head and a mumbled apology.

He shrugged and tucked his hands in his pockets.

"Figured." He sucked in a deep breath and let it out with another sigh. "I'm going to go. I'll see you for lunch sometime next week? As friends?"

"Friends."

He smiled at me, tight and unhappy, and he wandered away. I threw my ice cream in the trash on top of his and got in my car, grateful that I'd decided to drive myself rather than depend on Brian for a ride. I pulled into my driveway a few minutes later. The house was dark other than a light up in Fisher's room. Pocketing my house keys, I walked down the driveway and found myself heading up Gil's steps a few minutes later.

I hadn't been able to get him out of my head all night. All week. Since I met him, really. Gil was an addiction that I didn't want to shake. The rasp of his voice was a siren song pulling me in over and over. The way he looked at me like he was always halfway amused by me, but not in a way that made me feel bad about myself. Like he found me charming or, at the very least, worth looking at. Worth talking to.

Because we did manage to talk now and then between rounds of sex. But I wanted more. Because I was foolish and smitten and couldn't help myself even as I marched up to his front door and knocked.

"Can I come in?"

Gil perused me, his gaze raking up and down, making me feel exposed. "Yeah," he said. "Come on in."

I liked my house well enough, but I loved Gil's. Gil's house was decidedly lived in. From the rumpled blanket on the couch, to the way the remotes on the coffee table were scattered around haphazardly. Plus, it smelled like him. Like leather and ozone and home.

"Want a beer?"

"Not tonight." Tonight I didn't want anything that would prolong the inevitable. All I'd thought about tonight was him, and now that I was finally in his space, my low simmering want turned into a need so fierce it stole my breath.

I stepped up to Gil, slid into his personal space. My hands found his hips and I tilted my head up to look him in the eyes. He wasn't the easiest person to read. He kept himself pretty closed off a lot of the time, but I liked to tell myself that he was on the verge of opening up to me. I liked to pretend that we could make a go of it, even though he was terrified of that. Hell, so was I.

The last person I'd fallen for had been taken from me. It had been just Fisher and me for six long years. Part of me didn't know how to move on or how to fall for someone new. Another part of me already had.

I wasn't foolish enough to say any of this out loud. Instead, I closed my eyes and took what I was allowed. Rising on my toes, I brushed my mouth against his. My eyes squeezed tight and I wrapped my arms around him, pulling him flush against me. He came willingly, melting against me. Then, in the next breath, he took over. Sliding his tongue into my mouth, he kissed me in ways I'd only dreamt of being kissed.

He kissed me like he owned me. Like I belonged to him. And, maybe in these moments, it was true. And maybe it was enough. For now, it had to be. I had it in my mind to tell him about the date when I was walking up his driveway, then he'd opened the door and I knew the date didn't matter. It had been the biggest failure on the planet. All I'd thought about the whole time was that he wasn't Gil.

Brian didn't make me trip over myself with nerves. He didn't have that cutting sense of humor Gil had, or the smolder in his eyes when he looked at me. Or a million other things that made my pulse race.

Gil grabbed my ass and pulled me tight against him, grinding his cock against mine as he attacked my mouth. Something about Gil made me desperate. Needy. *Brave.* I didn't want to question it, not right in that moment with his tongue in my mouth and his fingers fumbling with my fly.

"Gil, wait," I said as he assaulted my neck with kisses and popped my fly open. Gil went still, like I'd hit the pause button on him or short-circuited his brain. His voice was rough and raspy when he spoke, thick with lust.

"Row?"

The way he shortened my name made me feel like that single syllable now belonged to him alone.

"I want your cock in my mouth," I said.

Gil gripped my hips and mouthed the shell of my ear. "I want you out of that shirt."

I loosened my bowtie with trembling fingers, meeting Gil's intense gaze while I worked at the knot.

"Keep the tie on."

"Okay," I agreed without question. Working the buttons of the shirt loose, I slid out of it. The bowtie hung loose and crooked around my throat, but the heat in Gil's eyes told me how much he appreciated the sight.

"On your knees then." He ghosted a kiss against my lips before waiting patiently for me to get on with it.

I was exposed. My pants hung open. My shirt was

gone. My bowtie was loose and crooked, reminding me of the fact that my chest was bare. I slid to my knees and fumbled with the fly of Gil's pants until it finally cooperated.

Gil slid his fingers through my hair and I leaned into his touch, seeking it out. I pulled his pants down to mid-thigh, wasting no time in freeing his cock. My mouth watered at the sight of him. God, he had an amazing cock. Thick and pretty, precum glistening on the tip, enticing me.

Moving in, I licked the drop of moisture off his cock, then flicked my gaze up to find him looking down at me. Brows furrowed, lips parted. He had a wild look in his eyes, like it was all he could do to stop himself from fucking my face. I wrapped a hand around the base of his cock and leaned in, laving my tongue over his balls before licking up the underside of his shaft.

Gil groaned and his hand tightened in my hair, anchoring me to him. Every tiny tug telling me without words that I was where I belonged. Where it made sense to be. Because Gil and I shouldn't make sense, but we did. A guy as handsome as him shouldn't want anything to do with someone off-balance and out of his depth the way I frequently was. But Gil moaned again when I took him in my mouth, a long drawn-out sound as he sank his other hand into my hair, cradling my head now. I didn't feel so clumsy or unsure suddenly. Instead I felt right and perfect, and like I was where I was meant to be.

My lips stretched around his cock and I used my tongue to tease the head. He tasted like skin, and salt, and I had to remind myself that I wouldn't get to keep this. Him. Gil had made it clear what he wanted and didn't want from me. Maybe this should be the last time I came over for this, I thought briefly, dismissing it as soon as the notion entered my head.

The truth was simple—I'd take as long as Gil would let me. I'd come over again. And again. And I'd keep coming over until he made me stop. Until he no longer answered the door and let me in and kissed me like he owned me and told me to get on my knees.

I jerked him as I sucked. Stroked and bobbed and made a mess of my face with my spit. Gil's hips stuttered as he tried not to thrust, but I liked it when he did. Knowing that I could undo him like this, that I could make Gil Valentine lose his mind made my cock throb.

Releasing his cock, I let my hands drop to my sides and I looked up at him, mouthful of cock, spit on my chin, loose bowtie still hanging on my neck. I must look like a complete slut. A wreck.

I had no pulse. No breath. I was sure I'd ceased to exist and that it was the look in Gil's eyes that ended me with its intensity.

"Do you want me to fuck your face, Row?" Gil caressed my cheek before sliding his hand back into my hair.

Unable to keep staring up at a man I wanted to keep forever, but knew I couldn't, I closed my eyes and took what he let me have.

He started slow and he talked while he leisurely used my mouth.

"That fucking bowtie, Rowan. I want to fuck you while you wear nothing but that. Want to gag you with it. Maybe I'll take it off and jerk your cock with it."

Gil's hips thrust harder. Deeper. His cock hit the back

of my throat and I choked around him. My cock throbbed in my pants, leaking and aching and desperate for me to touch myself. But I held off. I wanted to be desperate for him. I needed him to see how unhinged he made me feel.

Gil eased his tight hold on my hair, releasing a handful to push some strands off my face. "Maybe I'll make you come on your slutty little bowtie, and *then* I'll gag you with it."

I whimpered at the sound of that. Truthfully, I'd let Gil do anything he wanted to me. Anything at all. I'd let him suck me, fuck me, breed me, pin me down, tie me up, blindfold me, gag me. Hell, I'd let him keep me if he wanted. That's what I wanted most of all.

Desperation rose up in me like a tsunami wave rushing for the shore and I reached between my legs.

"Don't touch that cock, Rowan. That's mine."

I grabbed on to the top of his pants that were still around his thighs and held on for dear life. Because if I let go, I was going to shove my hand in my pants and it would just take the tiniest bit of friction to get me off. The fact that I'd whimpered when he laid claim to my cock should have mortified me, but I was too wound up, too drunk on Gil to care. Honestly, I liked the idea. I knew he only meant it in the heat of the moment. I wasn't his, as much as I wanted to be. But, for now, I could pretend.

CHAPTER 22
GIL

Rowan looked perfect.

On his knees with a mouthful of cock and that bowtie loose around his neck. I wanted to choke him with it, gag him with it, anything to stop him from getting me off with that sinfully hot mouth of his. Because I knew that, sooner or later, Rowan was going to come clean about his date. Even if it wasn't that night, it would be another night. I was on borrowed time with him, and it was nobody's fault but my own.

"Give me your hands," I rasped, grabbing both of his wrists in one hand above his head. Using his body, I walked us back to the wall, gritting my teeth at the way his eyes rolled back.

It was hard to believe sometimes I was the first man he'd been with because everything about Rowan was so perfectly made for being with another man. For being with me.

I found myself faced with the possibility that every time with Rowan could be the last time. And it was that fear that had me pulling my cock out of his mouth and replacing it with my fingers. It was that worry that had me stretching my hand toward the back of his throat until he choked up enough spit to make my fingers wet enough to get inside of him. Fisting the loose ends of his bowtie, I yanked him to his feet. He knew what to do, wrapping both of his legs around my waist.

I pressed Rowan against the wall, pressed two fingers into him, and dropped my forehead against his shoulder with a low groan. He shivered and whined, gyrating against the wall and fucking himself down onto my hand.

"Please," he whimpered. "I've been waiting to come to you all night."

"Come to me?" I asked, grazing my teeth across the side of his neck. "Or come for me."

"It's your cock," he rasped.

I replaced my fingers with my dick, notching the spit-soaked tip against his hole before letting gravity do its work. Rowan's asshole swallowed my cock as well as his mouth did, and I bared my teeth against his skin and bit him. Rowan moaned and flexed his thighs against my ribs.

"Mine," I murmured, thrusting upward into the tight heat of his body.

"Yours, Gil."

Long gone was the stuttering man who didn't know what to say to me to get what he wanted. Rowan was far more confident of himself now than he'd been weeks before on the first day he showed up in my driveway, frantic and frazzled.

Something about the impermanence of Rowan's presence in my life dropped a layer of urgency over the two of us, so I wasted no time reaching between our bodies. I yanked the bowtie off his neck and then took his cock into my fist. The patterned silk wrapped around his shaft, around my fingers, quickly getting wet from the precum I smeared over his length with every stroke. Rowan threw his head back, completely gone.

He was gone.

He'd be gone.

Soon.

"Is it still safe to come inside of you, Rowan?" I licked my way from his neck to his jaw to his ear. "I want to pump my load so deep into your ass you'll be dripping me out for days."

The sound that left his mouth was decadent, and it had me quickening the pace of not just my hips, but my hand. We'd barely gotten into the house before Rowan had made it clear what he wanted. Made it clear the one thing I was good for. His hands had moved for my waist like they had a home there, and foolishly I'd enjoyed the feel of him. He'd asked to suck my cock and I'd let him, the vision of his cherry red face and watery eyes forever emblazoned in my mind.

Long after Rowan—and Fisher—were gone, I'd still think of him.

I'd remember how close I'd come to having it all.

Rowan's body burned as his muscles tensed. His cock thickened in my hand, pulsing as he emptied onto his pretty little bowtie. The grip of his hole was like a vise, and it wasn't long before I followed after him. Jets of cum shot deep into his hole, and I fucked him so hard against the wall I worried his shoulder blades would dent the drywall. I cried out as I came, my cock so thick and hot it hurt to release. And it was Rowan's gentle hands at the small of my back that brought me back to myself.

"You possess me," I murmured against his ear, slowly lowering him down to the ground. His legs trembled, and I spun him quickly, pressing his chest against the wall and sinking to my knees behind him. I spread his cheeks apart with one hand and used his soiled bowtie to mop up the first drips of cum that leaked out of his well-fucked hole.

"Gil. Jesus." He thumped his forehead against the wall, and I used his tie and my tongue to clean him up. I know I'd threatened to shove the tie into his mouth, but I slipped it into my pocket instead. I didn't know if he noticed and I didn't really care. He was naked and I was still half-dressed, and it felt like the most appropriate metaphor for whatever this thing between us was turning into. Rowan, always eager and bare, not even realizing what he'd gotten himself into with me. And me, half-dressed, half-guarded…

I hooked my arm around Rowan's waist and pulled him down. His ass landed in my lap the same time my ass hit the floor, and the way he tucked his smaller body in against mine was everything I'd never known I wanted. Philip had never been a cuddler, and it wasn't until the first night I'd woken up with Rowan beside me, our legs tangled together, that I'd realized how much I wanted that kind of physical contact.

"Where's my bowtie?" Rowan asked, tracing a swirl over the top of my wrist with his fingertip.

"Around here somewhere."

He hummed.

"You should probably get home soon," I said, swallowing hard and trying to find the strength to get him off of me and out the door.

"I have some time," he answered back. "It's early and Fisher is asleep."

I wanted to tell him I sincerely doubted his son was asleep, but I bit it back. Rowan was the single parent and I was the one who'd never wanted kids. It was hardly my place to let him in on the things I'd noticed about his son.

Rowan shifted on my lap, stretching his naked body out on top of me like a cat. He yawned and stretched, and I let myself curl my hands around his waist. He fit so perfectly against every part of my body, it was impossible to ignore.

I didn't want to ignore it.

"Did you have company?" he asked, spine going rigid against my chest.

"Hmn?"

He pointed toward the coffee table, to Philip's gear that I'd never bothered to put away after our ride earlier in the evening.

"Your son was here again," I answered, shifting his weight on my lap.

"I'll tell him to stop bothering you so much."

He hadn't meant for the comment to hurt, but it cut me open just the same. I'd made it very clear to everyone in my life, to Philip, to Jack, and most recently to Rowan, what I thought about kids. And yet…Fisher was far from a bother.

"He's fine," I said softly. "Came by before dinner and asked for a ride."

Rowan's body went taut, and he shifted around on my lap so he could see my face. He was still flushed from the sex, his hair frazzled and the smallest beads of sweat that hadn't even had time to dry yet on his temple.

"It doesn't look like you told him no."

"I took him through town and brought him home." I bit the inside of my cheek. "Then he went home and got himself a pizza since you were on a date."

He scrambled off my lap like I'd bit him, and not in a sexy way.

"We never agreed that you could take him on your bike," he said.

I scoffed, the corner of my eye twitching hard enough to make my scar ache. "That's the part you're choosing to focus on? Alright, Row."

Rowan managed to get himself dressed in near record time, but I was slow to my feet. I hiked my pants up back around my waist, not bothering with the zipper.

"We just made a lap of the town and I brought him back."

"We had talked about a ride to school. Around the block or something. And that was a *strong maybe*, not a yes."

I scratched the back of my neck, debating if I wanted to give him back his bowtie or not. It burned a hole in my pocket, but I kept it there as he fumbled his way up the buttons of his shirt. I hadn't even bothered to look too hard at him upon his arrival, but Rowan had definitely dressed up for his date. He looked well and properly fucked now, though, and I smirked at the sight of him trying to tuck the tails of his shirt back into his pants.

"I kept it slow, Rowan. Jesus, you're being a little ridiculous right now."

"He's my son!" Rowan raised his voice, stabbing a finger into the middle of my chest. "He's my son, and he's all I have."

Fisher was all Rowan had because he definitely didn't have me. That was the quiet part that neither of us needed to say.

"It won't happen again."

"I know it won't."

Clearing my throat, I gestured to the front door. "You can go now."

He moved like he was going to do just that, but caught himself before his foot even hit the floor.

"No, I can't," he said.

"I assure you that you can." To demonstrate, I went to the door myself, and I opened it for him. The night air was getting far too crisp for comfort, and I dreaded the onset of fall into winter when it would be too cold to go out for a ride anymore. My bike was the fastest way for me to clear my head, and I hated not having that release available.

"I don't do well with arguments," he explained.

"Then don't start them."

He opened his mouth, eyes wide and bordering on angry, then he frowned and scrubbed a hand down his face. He almost wiped the expression clean, but the deep lines around the corners of his eyes were still there. At least...*I* could see them.

"He is my son," Rowan repeated. "And you are...you are..."

"I'm just a man who fucks you, Rowan," I said with a nod. "I know my place here."

"That's not what I meant."

"But it's the truth. Isn't it? You're a single dad and I'm just the guy around the block you found to pop your cherry."

"I'm trying to not argue with you," he said. "I don't want to leave angry."

"I'm not angry," I told him, and it was the truth.

I was resigned.

"Gil."

"This was a good wake-up call for both of us, don't you think?" I needed him to leave before I said something I couldn't take back. Before I told him that I liked him and that I didn't hate his son, and I wanted him to have a place in my bed whenever he wanted. I reached for him and pulled him near, closed the space between us until he was against my chest and his arms were around my waist. Maybe it was muscle memory. I kissed the top of his head and let out a breath, ruffling his hair.

"Yeah," he agreed, voice weak. "A wake-up call."

Maybe I'd been right to fuck him the way I had, to take him like it was going to be the last time. Because there in front of my door, the night air blowing around us, I thought I might have been right. Rowan was hesitant to go, though. I could feel it in the way his body swayed toward mine, even through his anger.

"Hey." I knocked my chin into the side of his head gently. "You never asked me about the accident where I got my scar."

Rowan tilted his head back, the flush in his cheeks gone, but his eyes now damp and ringed red.

"Tell me about the accident where you got your scar," he whispered.

I smiled and dipped down to kiss him, the softest

brush of my lips against the corner of his mouth. I hope he saw my question for the olive branch it was meant to be.

"It's getting late, Rowan." I kissed him again, again, again. "I'll tell you another time, alright?"

He licked his lips, pressing his fingers against the last place I'd kissed him.

"Alright," he agreed. "Another time."

CHAPTER 23
ROWAN

The argument with Gil left my insides feeling like crushed glass. If I thought about him for too long, my chest would squeeze and the pain threatened to undo me. So I didn't think about Gil. I went to work and ignored Brian, and everyone else for that matter. I worked through lunch hour and when I came home, I threw myself into finishing up the renovations in my bathroom.

Fisher was in a mood too, but every time I asked about it, he said he was fine. School was *fine*. His friends were *fine*. Everything was *fine*. He didn't need anything from me, so it would seem. He sulked around the house with his earbuds in, perfecting the whole moody teenager schtick.

The last thing I wanted to do was fight with Fisher, so I left him be. The fight with Gil still played on loop in my head despite my efforts to block it out. To forget it happened. I'd acted like an asshole. But he'd caught me off-guard by knowing about the date. I hadn't mentioned it and I wasn't sure I was going to.

The truth was that I didn't know how to bring it up without showing all my cards. Yes, I went on a date, but the whole time I was out with Brian, I wanted it to be Gil. I wanted him to pick me up and take me out. I wanted to go eat somewhere and then maybe go for a drive. Laugh. Talk. Kiss.

I wanted to hold his hand or snuggle up next to him in a theater. And dumping all that on him was hardly fair. He'd been crystal clear about his boundaries from the start. It was me who'd let his emotions run wild. It was me who'd gotten so invested in a man who liked me just fine enough to fuck me into oblivion, but didn't want more. And when he'd mentioned the date, he'd sounded completely unaffected by it, and I hated that. He might as well have been reading his grocery list for how much he cared that I'd gone on a date.

So maybe I'd blown things with the motorcycle out of proportion. Fisher had been excited about the ride, and I trusted Gil. He was good with Fisher. He took Fisher's moody teenage attitude in stride, but didn't take any of his shit. Fisher liked him.

I liked him.

Exhausted, I slumped down onto the floor of my bathroom and let out a deep breath. I still had so much work to do on the house. It was a never-ending list of things and for every task I crossed off, three more seemed to take its place. Watching Gil help Fisher with his bike unlocked all kinds of silly daydreams for me. Ones where I had someone rugged and handsome to help me fix broken things. But it was stupid of me to let myself go there, even briefly. It was Fisher and me against the world. And eventually he'd grow up and move on and it would just be me.

Before I could get too mired in my pit of loneliness, Fisher poked his head in the door. His hood was up, and his earbuds were in. He started to say something, then popped the earbuds out and held them in his hand. His brow furrowed.

"What is it, bud?"

"What's for dinner?" Fisher asked.

"What is there?"

Fisher shrugged. "You didn't go shopping."

Fuck. I hadn't. I was supposed to go a couple of days ago, but the thing with Gil had turned me inside out. Not that I could tell that to Fisher, though he wasn't stupid. He knew something was up, even if there was no way he'd know what exactly.

"I'll go now and I'll pick up some takeout on the way home. Did you want to come with me?"

Fisher thought about it for a moment, but shook his head. "Maybe next time."

"Sure, next time." I shot him a smile to show that I wasn't angry or upset and groaned as I got to my feet. Fisher stuffed his earbuds back in and disappeared upstairs to his room. We still had to paint up there, but he hadn't picked a color yet.

Maybe next weekend we could paint it together. It wasn't like I'd be sneaking down the street to see Gil anytime soon. It felt like a door had closed between us. Like a wall had been erected where there wasn't one before. And he stole my bowtie. I'd given the floor around us a cursory glance, but the bowtie hadn't been there.

I shouldn't like the idea of him keeping it, but I liked the idea that he was keeping a piece of me. All I had of him were the memories of the way he touched me. The way he said my name. His smile when he thought I couldn't see it and the way his mouth felt on mine. Memories of Gil were a bruise I couldn't stop pressing.

I took the long way around so I wouldn't have to drive by Gil's house. Pathetic, me? Probably. The grocery store was practically deserted when I'd arrived. Without a list to guide me, or a real idea of what we needed besides everything, I grabbed a cart and started at one end of the store.

I made sure to get some of Fisher's favorite snacks, as well as some pantry staples. All the work I'd done the past few days to outrun thoughts of Gil was catching up to me. Circling back around to the deli, I decided to grab something from there instead of making another stop for dinner on the way home.

I ordered a box of tenders and a couple sides of potato wedges. Tonight, ketchup could be the vegetable. Tomorrow I'd go back to being regular old Rowan. Responsible parent and functioning member of society. I just needed to sulk a little longer.

Turning to head to the registers, I came face to face with Brian. He looked far better than I felt.

"Rowan, how are you?"

"I'm good. Uh… just getting dinner. And a few things. How are you?" I cringed inwardly at how stupid I sounded. How stilted and fake. The worst part was that Brian didn't do anything wrong. I never should have agreed to go on the date in the first place. My feelings for Gil weren't something that I should have ignored. I should've walked away the first time I felt something more than lust simmer between us.

"About the other night…" I started to apologize when Brian lifted his hand, stopping me.

"Rowan, it's fine. You don't need to explain."

"I feel like I led you on." I shuffled my feet like an embarrassed teenager.

Brian shrugged. "Maybe I asked you out because I knew it wouldn't go anywhere. I mean, on paper, we're a good fit, but I knew at lunch that day that we'd be better friends." He shot me an apologetic look.

"I really am sorry, though. I'm kind of hung up on someone else."

Brian grinned at me, though he also seemed tired and a bit melancholy. "You and me both. Hey," he paused, looking a bit sheepish. "Can we still do lunch, though? As friends? I'm kind of short on those."

He ran a hand through his hair. "Wow, that didn't sound as pathetic in my head."

"Lunch would be nice. As friends. I don't exactly have a stacked social calendar myself." At least if we were both pitiful, it cancelled the other out.

"Great." Brian's smile seemed to come a little easier now that we'd established what a bad idea the date had been to begin with—on both our parts. Knowing he was also hung up on someone else made me feel better too. It reminded me that I wasn't alone in the world. That other people went through the same things I did.

After my wife died, it had felt that way for me. Like all I had left was Fisher. It was a hard mindset to break out of. I had to force myself to join parent groups at Fisher's school. I tried to stay plugged into the community and other people, but life as a single parent isn't easy. Eventually it became simpler to do my own thing. To just worry about Fisher and his quality of life. That was the thing to prompted the move. No matter what I did, life back in Crestview hadn't been easy on him.

Fisher seemed to have settled in well here. He had a few friends he hung out with at school and had even hung around with them after school a few times. It's all I wanted for him. A bit of happiness. A few friends. The guy down the road who taught him how to fix his bike had been a bonus. Gil was never part of the original plan. After all, how could he be? I hadn't known he existed, and even if I had, it wasn't like he was banging my door down, begging to be let in.

By the time I finished shopping, I was in a foul mood. I hated how stuck on Gil I was. How I had all these feelings swirling inside me like a storm with nowhere to go. They battered my insides until the whole of me felt tender and raw. And, of course, Brian was waiting for me outside the store.

"We meet again." I forced a smile, though I didn't know why I bothered. Brian knew I wasn't exactly in the sunniest of moods.

"I was halfway out of the parking lot when I turned around and came back to ask if we could trade phone numbers. And to ask if you're okay."

"I'll survive. But yeah, we can trade numbers." Instead of handing my phone over to Brian so he could put his number in, I did it myself. I wished that Gil and I were the kind of people who texted back and forth so at least I'd have had an old catalog of messages to scroll through when I couldn't get him out of my head. Instead, I had nothing. Just recollections of the way he looked at me when he opened his door. Like he was happy to see me and surprised about that fact, but willing not to question it too closely so he could kiss me. Because kissing me was necessary.

My imagination took liberties with the memories sometimes. Clearly I'd imagined things between us that were never there.

"Are you sure you're okay?" Brian asked again. "You can talk to me, you know."

"I know." I let out a sigh and sent Brian a text so he'd have my number in his phone. "But I have to get home and feed my kid."

"Okay. You owe me lunch, though." Brian looked like he had more to say, or ask, or that he wanted to press me again on my low mood, but thought better of it. "I'll see you around, Rowan."

"Yeah, see you." I watched Brian walk away for a few seconds before I headed for my car. After I unloaded the groceries, I was going to stuff my face with chicken tenders, then crawl into bed and pretend that tomorrow would be a better day.

CHAPTER 24
GIL

Saturday morning, I finally caved in.

Not about Rowan, but about Jack.

I showed up at his house with two breakfast burritos crammed into my backpack and what I hoped was an apology in my eyes. He opened the door looking tired, rubbing sleep from the corner of his eyes before stepping out of the way to let me in.

"You look like shit," I said.

He snorted. "My best friend has been blowing me off for a week and someone woke me up."

I slung the backpack onto one arm and unzipped it, wafting the smell of eggs and bacon in his general direction. It perked him up enough to smile, which was more than I deserved. Jack snatched the bag off my shoulder and shuffled off into the kitchen like a zombie only concerned with his next bacon fix.

"You look like shit too," he said, already with a bottle of hot sauce in hand.

I pressed my fingers against my jaw and rubbed at

the half-week's worth of scruff that had been growing since my fight with Rowan.

"I look like I haven't shaved. There's a difference."

Jack poked me beneath my eye, tracing his finger in a half-moon toward my temple.

"These bags are my imagination then?" he asked.

I swatted his hand away and stole the hot sauce, adding a generous sprinkle to the top of my own burrito before taking a bite and sliding onto a barstool.

"I haven't seen Rowan in a few days."

It was the truth, but my issues were so far beyond simply *not* seeing him. It was more than just the sex too. I'd gone two years after Philip without being intimate with another man, but a handful of weeks with Rowan had made the thought of another two near impossible. I also knew that didn't have anything to do with the act itself, but more the person I was engaging in the act with. It was Rowan who had caught me in his net and stole me for himself. Whether he'd meant to or not didn't matter. He and his damn kid had worn on me, and even just three days in…I missed them both.

"So, fighting with everyone who cares about you?" he asked around a mouthful of a breakfast he hadn't even paid for.

Sighing, I took another bite of my breakfast. "When is the wedding?"

"The spring." He added more hot sauce to both of our burritos, more for mine and less for his. Just like always.

"I know what you said last time we talked." The foil wrapper crinkled loudly beneath my fingers. "That our friendship—"

He cut me off, smacking me on the side of the head with so much force I almost fell off the barstool. "You know what you thought you heard, not what I said."

"You said they didn't think you should stand up for him if we were friends," I repeated it to him. I remembered exceedingly well what he'd said to me.

"Right." He bit into his burrito, eyeing me over the top edge, eyes finally awake and somewhat amused.

"I shouldn't be here. I just…"

"Why not?" he asked, tilting his head to the side. "Why shouldn't you be here?"

"Because Philip is your brother. They're your family."

"You're more family to me than any of them have ever been." Jack set his burrito down, propped against a fruit bowl, and hit me again…this time in the middle of my chest.

I rubbed the contact point, even though it hadn't hurt. I was too stunned for pain. "What do you mean?"

"He's my brother. They're my parents, but…you're my best friend."

"Jack." I set my breakfast down beside his, rubbing my greasy hands off on the thighs of my jeans.

"I'm not going to stand up for him as long as he's lying to everyone about who he is," he said softly.

"He's not gay," I reminded. "He's always been bisexual. Like me. It's fine for him to be with a woman. He's not lying."

"He doesn't want to marry her, though. She's sweet, but she's not right for him and he knows it. He's told me so. He just wants everyone off his back." Jack dragged his tongue across the front of his teeth and shrugged, doing everything he could to avoid my gaze. "And I won't support that. It's not fair for either of them. Or me."

"Or you?"

Jack's cheeks flushed red as the hot sauce between us.

"If they push it on him, they'll push it on me, and I'm…I'm not as good of a liar as he is," Jack admitted.

"Are you…are you coming out to me right now?"

He scrubbed both hands down his face and walked to the other end of his kitchen, staring out the window over of his sink.

"I don't know what I'm doing. I'm just saying, I can't—no—I *won't* stand up for him. I won't support what he's doing or what they're asking of him."

"Have you told them yet?" I asked, turning to study the tight lines of his back, muscles stretching the thread-bare t-shirt I was fairly certain he'd stolen from me at some point in our friendship.

"That I wouldn't stand up, yeah."

"When?"

"Before I talked to you last."

Regret exploded in my stomach, souring the cheese and eggs that had already begun to settle there.

"I'm a shit, Jack." I climbed off the stool and went to him, turning him around and wrapping my arms around him. Jack sighed and pressed his forehead against my shoulder, arms hanging limp at his sides.

"You're fine," he muttered into my chest.

"I should have been here for you. For whatever you needed."

"It was complicated." He sighed again and shrugged his shoulders to knock me loose. I let him go, taking a step back so I could see his face.

"Are they speaking to you still?"

"Philip is, but our parents aren't. Though, I think if I told them everything I told you, he'd cut me out too."

"Do you want to talk about this? Any part of it?"

I'd been a horrible friend. After Philip and I split up, Jack had saved me from myself in ways I'd never be able to thank him for, and the first time he truly needed me since then, I was so wrapped up in my own head and my own shit that I hadn't even known what he was going through. Rowan—and my feelings for him—had tripped me up beyond comprehension, and I'd very nearly lost the person who mattered more than anyone else.

"No," he said simply. "I just want you to know that I choose you, and if I ever want to talk about the rest of it—"

"I'm here," I said, shoving my hands into my pockets. "I'll always be here."

"And you'll listen better," he added, mouth twitching into a smirk. "So you hear what you're being told, not what you think is being said."

"I'll listen better," I promised him.

"Okay." Jack's stomach growled, and he glanced longingly back at our abandoned breakfast. "Can you move so I can get my burrito?"

I stepped out of the way and followed Jack back to the bar, climbing onto the stool and re-saucing both of our burritos. We ate together in a quiet and companionable silence which felt more comfortable than any other feeling I'd had since the middle of the week.

After we finished and I gathered my helmet and backpack to get ready to head back home, Jack stopped me in the hallway with a gentle touch on my forearm.

"There's one more thing," he said.

I swallowed down all the garbage feelings that had churned up earlier in the morning, hoping I didn't know what was going to come next.

"I don't want to see him, Jack."

"You don't have to."

"I don't want to talk to him either," I said.

"Maybe just to clear the air," he said.

"It's already polluted," I said, sliding my helmet over my head in hopes having half my face obscured would keep Jack off my case. "There's nothing more for Philip and I to say to each other."

"Are you sure?"

Before I could argue, he reached up and slammed my visor closed. He furrowed his brow, and clicked it back open.

"What?" I asked, rolling my eyes at him.

"You didn't say what was going on with Rowan."

"Nothing is going on with Rowan." I closed my visor again.

"That's different from before."

"Rowan was always just a distraction," I reminded Jack, adjusting my backpack into place on my shoulders and sidestepping toward his front door.

"You fell in love with him," Jack said.

"No."

"Yes," he argued.

"I don't love Rowan Verne."

But it was a lie. I could taste it in the back of my throat.

"Don't make his kid the issue, Gil."

"I didn't come over here to talk about Rowan," I

pointed out. "I came over here to talk about you and me and your brother."

"Is it not an extension of that?"

"Not today, Jack, alright?" I opened his front door and stepped onto the porch.

"Tomorrow, then," he said.

"You know Sunday is my alone day."

"Tomorrow, then," he repeated.

The thought of going home and knowing Rowan wouldn't be showing up at my house in the middle of the night soured what was left of the tolerable feelings that lived in my body, and I answered Jack with a reluctant nod.

"Tomorrow."

"Your Sunday isolation rule is ridiculous anyway," he said, closing the door halfway on me. "You don't need to sulk alone."

Suddenly, it was hard to breathe, hard to see. Was I about to cry? That was preposterous. My scar ached, and even though I had the visor down, I turned away quickly so Jack couldn't see.

"Tomorrow!" he hollered as I shoved the key into the ignition on my bike. "And thanks for breakfast!"

I turned the bike on, the roar of the engine drowning out whatever he was about to say next. I didn't deserve Jack's forgiveness, at least not as quickly as he'd given it. But that was the thing about Jack, why he'd always been the best man in his family. Why he'd always been the best man in my life. I took the long way back home, winding around the edges of town. Somehow, I knew what was coming next, but I was out of back roads and I needed coffee before I lost my mind. I needed to get home, even though I knew with certainty who would be there when I pulled into the driveway.

I opened the garage and pulled in alongside my car, cutting the ignition and resting the bike on its stand. I took my helmet off without looking behind me, but the familiar click of Fisher's bicycle kickstand hitting the concrete was unmistakable. How quickly he and his dad had ingrained themselves into my life.

"What do you want, Fisher?" I yanked my helmet off and rested it on the fuel tank.

"Something's wrong with my bike," he said, pulling his earbuds out and sliding them into his pocket. He looked so much like how I imagined Rowan must have looked at that age. Curly red hair and bright blue eyes, freckles across his cheeks, and limbs too long for his body. Even with the hoodie pulled up over his head, it was impossible to ignore the vibrant shock of curls that poked out, and I found myself wondering what his mother looked like.

"Does your dad know you're here?" I asked.

"He's been working on the house non-stop all week," Fisher said. "He forgot to get groceries yesterday and he's just…I don't know."

"That wasn't an answer."

"He told me not to bother you anymore."

"And yet."

"I'm not bothering you, though. Am I, Gil? I don't think I am."

I shrugged out of my backpack and unzipped my leather jacket, frowning down at the most earnest and brave kid I'd ever met in my life. I couldn't walk away from him and his dad, just like I couldn't walk away from

Jack. I'd repaired one of the relationships in my life, and whether I wanted it or not…Rowan was going to be up next. Even if I never got him into my bed again, we needed to have a proper conversation about what had happened between us and what the future of our relationship looked like. Not just for us, but for Fisher too.

Notwithstanding, that third party was one of the reasons I'd been so adamantly against kids in my relationship with Philip…but Fisher was a barnacle I hadn't yet been able to shake. Sighing, I stared down at him, seeing so much of Rowan in his face I knew I couldn't turn him away.

"What's wrong with the bike, kid?"

CHAPTER 25
ROWAN

Fisher had been gone for an awful long time. It wouldn't have been a big deal except that he was supposed to have chosen a paint color so we could start on his room this weekend. Every time I turned around this week, he was on his bike, or tinkering with his bike. That was definitely Gil's influence.

Ever since Fisher met him, he'd been borderline obsessed. Gil was the kind of cool guy that any kid would love to have as a dad. Whereas I was a nerdy mortgage broker who wore bowties and whose idea of working on a car was driving it to the mechanic.

It wasn't that Fisher and I didn't have anything in common. We shared a love of the same kind of movies. We had the same sense of humor and enjoyed the same books for the most part. But Fisher's new interest in wrenches and bike parts was definitely not my doing.

I'd told Fisher not to bother Gil. It didn't seem right to let my kid go over there all the time and be a nuisance if Gil and I weren't… whatever. We hadn't been anything before and we weren't anything now. It was definitely rude for me to let my kid go over there and stalk Gil in his garage. Because I knew without going down the street that Fisher was there and he wasn't happy with me.

I sent Fisher a text telling him that I needed him home. I stared at my phone waiting to see if he'd even looked at it or not before sending another one.

Fisher answered after the second text, promising to be home soon.

How soon was soon, I asked. Fisher sent a shrugging emoji.

Theoretically, I could go down the street and drag him home. But that would mean seeing Gil, and I wasn't sure I was ready for that. I'd staunchly avoided him since the last weekend because I knew I'd gotten in over my head with him and it was my own fault. Gil had been honest from the outset that we were sex and not a single thing more. It was my own greedy heart that had latched on to the idea of him. If only he'd been terrible to Fisher, I'd have a reason to cut him out without a second thought. But Gil was good to him, and good with him. He was patient and kind and he'd cared about my input.

Yeah, I'd gone off at the fact that he took Fisher on his bike, but I'd been looking for a reason to be mad at him because then I couldn't be mad at myself. My desire to have more with him had been foolish, but I'd let myself daydream about it anyway. Even on the date with Brian, all I'd thought about was Gil. And it would seem that my kid also thought highly of him.

Fisher came inside a half an hour later, by which point my nerves were frayed.

"You weren't bothering Gil, were you?"

Fisher had barely walked in the door before the words were out of my mouth.

He shrugged. "He said I wasn't."

"I asked you not to go over there." The last thing I wanted was for Fisher to have his feelings hurt if Gil decided one day that he didn't want his former fuck buddy's kid hanging out in his garage.

"It's not a big deal."

"It is to me. I asked you not to do something and you did it anyway."

"Because you're being stupid. Gil likes me. He's nice to me."

"I know you like Gil, but I'd rather you didn't bother him anymore. If I find out you've been over there again, I'll ground you."

"That's stupid," Fisher snapped. "It's not fair."

No, it wasn't fair. In a perfect world, Gil would care for me the way I'd come to care for him. In a perfect world, he'd spend the night here and wake up in the morning and we'd eat breakfast, the three of us. We'd go on dates and hold hands in public. Silly things that couples did.

"No, it's not fair. But it's the rule."

"It's a stupid rule," Fisher spat. Suddenly, he was the old Fisher. The angry pre-move Fisher who'd railed at anything and everything because of the emotional turmoil he'd been put under at school.

"I know you're not happy, Fish," I started to say, but he cut me off.

"I was happy, though. You dragged me all the way out here and yeah, no one picks on me because I don't know anyone. But Gil took me on his bike and he teaches me shit, and he's cool. He's my friend."

"I know you don't understand, and I'm sorry, but what I say goes."

Fisher's expression was thunderous. Murder glinted in his gaze and, for the first time in his life, his temper flared hot enough to justify the stereotype of the angry redhead.

"What you say is stupid!" Fisher flung the door open and glared back at me. "You don't want me to have any friends."

"Fisher, that's not true." I started for the door, but he was off like a shot. My heart clenched in my chest, squeezing tight, not beating.

"I hate you!" Fisher tore out of the driveway on his bike, peddling for all he was worth. His helmet dangled from the handlebars as he sped away. I tried to chase after him, but he was too fast.

"Fisher! Fisher, come back!" I knew he wouldn't. He wouldn't turn around and come back. He hated me. I'd fucked everything up and now Fisher hated me.

Gil hated me.

Everyone hated me.

I went inside and tried to keep busy, but mostly I paced back and forth and looked out the window every two minutes, waiting for my son to return. I hated fighting with him, and he knew what it did to me when we left things unresolved. The worst of it was that I only had myself to blame.

One hour into Fisher's vanishing act and the fear really started to set in. I'd tried to play it cool at first, telling myself that he'd be home any minute. But when an hour turned into an hour and a half, worry turned to panic. I'd tried his phone, but it kept going to voicemail. He'd clearly switched it off.

My chest squeezed so tight it was hard to draw a full breath. I thought about getting into my car to look for him, but I was halfway down the street before I realized what I was doing. Stopping for a breath, I put my hands on my knees and tried to calm myself. I could see Gil's house from where I was. The garage door was open and it felt like an omen. An invitation.

I ran toward that door, my heart in my throat. My brain didn't want to be reasonable. I knew that the likelihood of history repeating itself were slim to none, but I was irrationally terrified that something horrible was going to happen. Fear climbed into my veins and made my body tremble.

I stumbled up Gil's driveway and hurled myself into his garage.

"Gil! Gil! He's gone. Fisher. Gil, I can't." It was like I was having an out-of-body experience at this point. I was looking down on myself, knowing that I was being irrational and emotional, but unable to put the brakes on myself.

Gil appeared from under the hood of the car that never left the garage. "What do you mean, gone? He was just here."

"We fought. Oh, God. We fought and he hates me and he left angry, and we're not supposed to do that. We can't leave angry."

Gil came to me and put his hands on my arms. Gripping me by the shoulders, he stared into my eyes. "Rowan, deep breath."

Right. Oxygen. I followed his lead and sucked a deep breath in. He had me let it out slowly. After the third one, I was slightly calmer, though still frantic, just more composed.

"Gil, we fought. He hates me. He's so mad at me."

"Kids get mad at their parents. It's the law."

"His mother. His mother… the night she died. We fought. We fought so bad and she left, and we never got a chance to put things right or say we were sorry. Gil, I can't… I can't lose him. I've lost everyone I care about. I lost my parents, and his mom, and now you. I can't lose him too. He's been gone for over an hour and he's not answering texts or calls. I go straight to voicemail."

Gil guided me to a five-gallon bucket that he'd over-turned. I'd seen Fisher use it for a stool before and Gil plonked my ass down on it.

"Sit here. I'll go look for him." Gil was already on his bike and was shoving his helmet on before it registered that he was going to jump in and look for Fisher for me. On another day, I might have been more equipped to deal with Fisher's rebellion, but it had been a long week with no sleep. I worked my day job, then came home and did renovations until nearly midnight some nights. Only to tumble into bed and toss and turn half the night.

Physically, I was exhausted, but emotionally, I was eviscerated. I'd already been hanging on by a thread when Fisher came home covered in dirt from tinkering in Gil's garage with him. Not only had Fisher done the one thing I asked him not to, but he'd been right about me being stupid. His friendship with Gil should have been more important than my feelings.

When I realized that I didn't know how long I'd been

sitting on the bucket in Gil's garage, I got to my feet and searched the garage and found an old envelope. I scrawled a note on the back telling Gil I'd gone home to wait for Fisher there and left it on the bucket I'd been perched on. I pulled the garage door shut as I left. For all I knew, Fisher might have gone home while I sat in a fog in Gil's garage. The short walk felt like it was ten miles and when I got there, Fisher was still nowhere to be seen. His bike was still gone, but I checked the whole house and the back yard anyway.

It hit me how big and empty my house was without Fisher in it. Even when he was hibernating in his room, being anti-social, his presence offered comfort. I fled the house in favor of standing at the end of the driveway, looking up and down the street. I squinted, trying to make out if any mopey teenagers were making their way back to me. I strained to hear the familiar rumble of Gil's bike, but I was met with nothing but the wind rustling and the odd car horn off in the distance.

I pulled out my phone and sent a flurry of text messages to Fisher.

I love you
I'm sorry
Come home and we'll talk about this
I'm not mad
Fisher, please come home
Fisher, I'm worried
I love you

After I sent the last one, I sank down and sat on the curb. Part of me wanted to go look for him, but the other part of me knew that I shouldn't get behind the wheel when I was one wrong move away from a full-blown anxiety attack. The familiar band of stress had wrapped around my chest the minute Fisher stormed out and I knew it wouldn't let go until he came home.

Because he would come home. I refused to catastrophize.

He had to come home.

CHAPTER 26
GIL

had lapped town twice, gone up and down every side street and back alley and there was no sign of Fisher. I didn't know how long he'd been missing for, and I didn't think he would have been ballsy enough to go past the city limits, so against my better judgement, I headed back to the house. Rowan wasn't there, which was surprising and not at the same time. The garage door was closed and the upturned bucket was still beside the wheel well of the Cougar where I'd last left him.

Rolling the bike into the garage, I cut the ignition and yanked off my helmet, cursing under my breath when I realized my fingers were shaking. I was worried about Rowan. I hadn't seen a lot of Rowan besides when he was in my bed or bent over his own couch, but I'd never seen him as amped up and frantic as he'd been when he showed up at my house screaming about his missing son. And it wasn't just Rowan who had me out of sorts. It was Fisher too, I realized. I was scared for Rowan's missing son, and when the fuck had that happened? When had I started to care about Rowan's kid as much as I'd started to care about him?

It was my turn to collapse onto the bucket, head in my hands and scar rough against my palm. For so long I'd been adamant, no kids, no kids, no kids. It was the only reason Philip and I had split up. Or if not the only reason, a main one. His family would have driven us apart eventually, but there'd been a good stretch of time when I liked to imagine our love was stronger than their hate. We could have made it through anything, if only we wanted to, but Philip was willing to pander to his parents and I wanted no part in that.

So maybe, I realized, it wasn't that I hadn't wanted kids.

I simply hadn't wanted kids with him.

"Fuck."

I pulled my phone out of my pocket to call Rowan, but as soon as I had the device in my hand, I realized I couldn't. We'd never exchanged phone numbers, never even sent a text. Our entire relationship was based on late night door knockings and quietly taking our clothes off so we didn't wake Fisher up…so we had more time. And we had our ridiculous rules that kept him far enough away I wouldn't fall in love with him, but it was probably too late for that too.

Wasn't it?

I didn't need to have taken Rowan Verne on dates to know I loved him. I loved the way he melted against me when we kissed, and I loved the way he didn't ever want to leave angry—even if I hated the reason for it. I loved the way he loved his son, how he would put himself at a disadvantage to give Fisher the best of everything, to put himself at a disadvantage to give me the best of him. Though what I had of Rowan was far from whole, it was more than enough for me to know I wasn't going to lose him over my own lost ideals about what I wanted in life, and I sure as shit wasn't going to lose him to a choad named Brian.

I was seconds away from tugging my helmet back on and heading around the block to his house when Rowan's car came barreling around the corner, skidding to a stop in front of my driveway.

"Did you find him?" I asked, discarding the helmet on the bucket and jogging down the driveway.

"He's at the hospital." Rowan choked on the words, barely more than a wet sob.

"Okay." One of us needed to be cool, and it definitely wasn't Rowan. Though, tears pricked the corners of my eyes as well, I fought to hold them back. I needed to be strong for Rowan…

For both of them.

"Slide over," I said, heading for the driver's side of the car. "You shouldn't be driving."

He didn't argue, hauling himself awkwardly over the console to make room for me, but lord was he short. I adjusted the seat back enough to make room for my legs, used the app on my phone to close the garage door, then headed toward the hospital.

"What happened?" I asked after we made it around the corner.

"I don't know for sure." Rowan was trembling like a leaf, curled in over himself with worry.

"Put your seatbelt on, Rowan."

He yanked the strap across his chest, struggling to get

the clip into the latch. I came to a stop at a red light and reached over, taking it out of his hands and sliding the two pieces together with ease. His fingers were clammy, and his face streaked with tears. I took both of his hands in mine and raised them, dusting kisses across his knuckles, then gently tracing wetness from the curve of his nose. Someone behind me honked, and I saw the light had turned green. I gave them the finger for good measure, then returned my hands to the steering wheel.

"Is he…" I trailed off, not brave enough to ask the question.

"He's fine," Rowan said, a wet laugh gurgling out of his throat. "I should have opened with that."

"It's okay," I told him, relief washing over me like waves in the ocean. "I was worried too."

"He wrecked his bike," Rowan explained. "The police said—"

"The police?"

"He wrecked his bike and got hurt. Someone found him and called the cops. The cops called the ambulance. I got the call once they got him to the hospital."

"How hurt?"

"They said he's stable and to come down," he muttered. "That's all I know."

"All of that's good."

I reached over the console and grabbed Rowan's thigh, using him to anchor myself for the last few minutes of the drive. He covered my hand with his, dropping his head against the headrest and closing his eyes. I glanced over at him as I pulled into the parking lot, finding him calmer than he'd been before, but still actively crying.

I needed to tell him how I felt about him, the words so urgent it hurt to keep them in, but I knew it wasn't the right time or the right place. He wouldn't even hear me over the rush of his own fear, and what if I woke up the next morning and didn't feel the same? Maybe this was all adrenaline confusing me and making me think I was in love with Rowan Verne when it was just the fight or flight kicking itself on.

Even as I parked the car and followed Rowan into the emergency room, I knew that was a lie. I was hopelessly in love with him, and one good sleep wasn't going to change that.

I hung back while he gave his information to the nurse at the desk, hesitant to try and come after him because I wasn't family. But Rowan reached behind him and took my hand before I could finish the thought. He pulled me down the hallway and around the corner, past a row of curtains until we reached a bed on the end that held his son, looking smaller and more scared than I'd ever seen him.

Fisher's relief when he saw his dad, and then me, was the straw that broke me. I shook free of Rowan's hand and covered my face, turning my back to the bed so neither of them saw me cry. Fisher's arm was in a sling and he had a nasty scrape across his cheek, but other than that…

He was alive.

I pressed my finger and thumb against my scar, one against the top and the other against the bottom, tapping until my heart rate slowed. It was an old habit from the early days after my accident, when I wanted to measure the distance of my disfigurement. It never grew and it never shrunk. Instead it was a permanent reminder of the night I'd almost lost my life because I let my emotions get the better of me.

Swallowing heavily, my limbs began to tingle. My adrenaline was finally starting to crash. I left Rowan and Fisher alone in their curtained-off room and found a chair in the hall, collapsing into it before my knees gave out. I fell forward, resting my elbows on my knees, taking deep breaths to manage the anxiety that had already begun to creep up from the base of my spine. Another technique I learned after the accident, one my therapist recommended because nightmares kept me up at night.

I closed my eyes and focused on my breathing, losing track of time, ignoring the smell of sanitizer, and the uncomfortable arms of the chair digging into my hips. I got so lost in my own head, I didn't hear Rowan come out for me.

"Hey," he said gently, fingers tentatively working through my hair.

Without looking up, I reached for his wrist, giving him a squeeze.

"He's okay?" I asked.

Rowan hummed, sounding so much more at peace than he had when we'd gotten to the hospital.

"Broken arm that they're going to cast now that I'm here," he said. "Some road rash on his face. A sprained finger."

Slowly I lifted my head, keeping Rowan's hand in place so I could kiss his fingers when my mouth made it to his hand.

"I'm glad," I whispered against his ring finger.

Rowan huffed and licked his lips. "He's asking to see you."

"What?"

He nodded.

"He specifically said to me *I want to talk to Gil now.*"

There weren't words that would ever encompass the way that made me feel, so I didn't try to find any. I simply nodded and let Rowan walk me back into the curtained cubicle.

"Hey, Fish," I said. "Gave your dad quite a fright."

He shrugged, then whimpered. Rowan went to him, sitting on the edge of the bed and fussing over the way the sling rested against his chest.

"Dad said you went and looked for me."

I nodded.

"Did you find my bike?" he asked.

"No. Did the cops take it when they brought you in?"

"I don't think so."

"Where is it?" I asked. "I'll go get it."

Fisher frowned, looking far younger than twelve. "I don't think we'll be able to fix it."

"I can fix anything," I assured him.

Rowan looked at me and smiled softly, and I hoped he knew I didn't just mean that about the bike. I could fix anything, and I *would* fix anything. I'd fix everything, especially my relationship with the two of them.

"It's up near the top of the vista," he said, and an unexpected bubble of anger bloomed and exploded in the middle of my chest.

"The vista?" My voice was louder than it should have been, but Fisher needed to know how stupid that was.

"There's too many cars up there. The roads are too winding. You could have…"

"My dad already told me all this," he said, and Rowan glared at him for good measure.

"You're lucky to be alive," I rasped.

"My dad said that too."

I took a step back and let out a breath, bracketing my hands around my waist so I didn't strangle the kid in front of me. That felt like a very not fatherly thing to do, and I wondered how our relationship was going to change once Rowan and I got serious with each other. Of course, assuming Rowan even *wanted* to get serious with me. We'd both been in agreement about what things were supposed to be, and he might not want…

Oh, God, what if he didn't want me?

"What did you want to ask him?" Rowan said softly, brushing Fisher's hair away from his face.

"If you'd go get my bike," he said. "I lost an earbud up there too."

He held up one of his hands, one white bud in his palm.

"I'll go look," I told him, "But I wouldn't have high hopes for the earbud, kid."

"Aw, man."

"You never even have music on anyway," I reminded him, rolling my eyes.

"Wait." Rowan looked from Fisher to me, and back to Fisher. "What?"

That wasn't a conversation for me, so I checked my pocket for Rowan's car keys. "Are you good if I take your car to go get his bike? I'll come back and hopefully he'll be all casted and we can get you two home."

"Home?" Rowan asked, almost to himself before nodding and clearing his throat. "Yeah. Thanks, Gil. That sounds good."

"Alright." I gave them both one last look, wanting more than anything to wrap them both in my arms, and then in bubble wrap, but deciding instead to turn away without another word. Just in case I said something I couldn't take back.

CHAPTER 27
ROWAN

Even with Fisher sitting there, alive and safe, if a little banged up, my adrenaline still surged through my veins like I was in the middle of a rollercoaster without a seatbelt and I had to rely on physics and sheer stubbornness to keep myself from flying off the track.

With Gil gone, I suddenly felt unmoored and I sank into the chair next to the bed. My left leg immediately started bouncing and I quickly stood back up.

I couldn't talk about the fight or the way I felt when he took off. Or the way my chest had caved in when the hospital called me to tell me they had my son in the emergency room. The veneer of composure I wore was thin, fragile, and ready to break.

"Tell me about the earbuds," I said. It was a safe topic. Something easy to approach my son about.

"If you tell me about Gil." Fisher had the audacity to notice that we'd come in together, me holding onto Gil's hand like he was the only thing keeping me standing.

"Tell me about the earbuds." I shoved my hand through my hair, raking my fingers over my scalp to help ground myself.

Fisher glanced away, then looked down at the singular earbud he had left. "It started at the other school. Before we moved. People will say all kinds of shi—stuff to you, and around you, if they think you can't hear them."

Gently, I sat down on Fisher's bed, on the side with his good arm. "And you felt you needed to play spy master?"

Fisher shrugged, then winced. "Sometimes they'd leave me alone if they thought I couldn't hear them. Sometimes it made them louder. But it felt like protection. I know it doesn't make sense."

"It doesn't have to. We all have our own different coping mechanisms."

Fisher glanced at me, a smirk on his still too-pale face. "Like endless home repairs."

"It was a fixer-upper. You knew that."

"Dad, come on. You'd come home from work, eat, then spend the rest of the night painting and whatever. I have earbuds. You have grout."

"So all those times I thought you couldn't hear me, you were actually ignoring me?"

"I can't be too good. I have to give you some grief."

I looked down at his busted arm and the painful-looking road rash on his face. "Maybe a little less grief next time, okay?"

Fisher nodded. "I'm sorry I took off. I knew when I did it that it would fu—upset you."

"I'm just glad you're okay."

"Are *you* okay?"

"I've been better, Fish. Honestly been a lot better."

"You have to tell me about Gil now."

"I'm not sure what there is to tell." Gil had looked just as stricken as I'd felt when I told him about Fisher and the call from the hospital. He'd looked for my son for me. Clearly, he cared about Fisher, but that was because Gil was a good person. Good people cared about shit like missing and injured kids.

Fisher rolled his eyes. "You can tell me why if you like Gil so much, you went on a date with that other guy?"

Suddenly, I was faced with a very grown-up sounding kid. I didn't know how to explain that Gil and I were just sex, and nothing more, though I wanted him in every single way that I could have him. And seeing him drop everything for Fisher, for me, really drove home the fact that not only did I want Gil, but I was terrifyingly in love with him.

He was patient with my son. And Fisher loved him. He'd loved him right from that first day he'd wandered up to Gil's house and asked for help with his bike. Fisher was just a kid, and kids got attached to people easily. It was part of the reason I hadn't dated much. It felt too risky to bring people around Fisher in case he got attached and things didn't work out. It was also a good reason for me to not date. For years I hadn't been interested in any of it. I'd even convinced myself at one point that I'd be happy being alone forever.

And it might have been true at that time. And then I'd met Gil Valentine.

"Sometimes, adults do things that don't make sense for reasons they convince themselves do make sense."

Fisher wrinkled his nose. "That's stupid."

Laughing, I agreed with him. "I know. It was stupid. For a lot of reasons."

"Because you like Gil."

"Because I like Gil." It was impossible not to agree with him. I liked Gil. I more than liked Gil. Saying I liked Gil was like looking at an ocean and calling it a puddle. Inadequate at best, ridiculous at worst.

"So why didn't you go on a date with Gil, instead of sneaking around when you think I'm sleeping?"

I blinked at Fisher. "Excuse me?"

"Dad, you're not a master spy yourself or anything. I'd no sooner turn my light off and you were out the door."

"You were supposed to be asleep." I ran my hand through my hair again. Somehow, when I wasn't looking, my son had grown up. He wasn't a little kid anymore and I had to stop pretending he was. I owed it to him to be honest.

"I went out with Brian because I didn't think Gil wanted to go out with me. Our relationship wasn't supposed to include that. I will always miss your mom, but meeting Gil showed me that maybe I'm ready to move on. If you're okay with that. I don't want to rush you or do anything you're not going to be comfortable with."

"I like Gil," Fisher said.

Our conversation was cut short when a doctor came in to put the cast on Fisher. He explained that they'd already taken x-rays and once the cast was on they'd take another set to make sure everything was lined up the way it should be.

The road rash on his face was superficial and should heal with little to no scarring, something Fisher almost looked sad about. To which I raised my eyebrow.

"What?" he said, obviously embarrassed that I'd noticed his disappointment. "Gil's scar is badass."

It was pretty hot, I had to admit. But I didn't have to admit that to Fisher.

"You're lucky you got off so easily. You could've been hurt a lot worse." My voice wavered, despite me trying to keep it steady. But I was having an increasingly hard time holding myself together.

"I know." Fisher's voice was small and riddled with guilt. "I'm sorry I took off. I did it because I knew it would hurt you."

It had been like living through my worst nightmare all over again. It was bad enough when I lost his mom. There was no way I'd have survived losing Fisher.

"You're okay. That's the most important thing."

"My bike is ruined." Fisher looked pretty devastated about that.

"I'm sure Gil will help you fix it. He said he can fix anything." I hoped he meant it. Because now that Fisher was okay, I wanted Gil and me to be okay. My heart was full of wants and desires, of dreams for how my life could look. Should look. Because, to me, Gil belonged to us. To Fisher and to me.

In truth, I didn't know him well. I knew he had good taste in beer and cars. I knew if it had tires, he could fix it. I knew other things about him too. Like the way it felt when he pulled me against him, and how it made me feel like he'd do anything to protect me. I knew that he was strong enough to carry me, to pin me down, and that his grip was like iron. I knew what he looked like when he was trying not to smile, and what he looked like when he didn't think anyone was watching him.

Like the way he'd crumbled when he saw Fisher in that hospital bed.

I knew enough of Gil to know that I wanted to know more. Know everything. The story behind his scar. How he met his best friend. I wanted to know his past and to be a part of his future.

When Fisher and I returned from x-ray a second time, Gil was waiting for us. He shot to his feet when I wheeled Fisher into the curtained-off area.

Gil took a look at Fisher's cast and his complexion turned a little green, but he managed a smile. "How's the arm?"

"Hurts. How's my bike?"

Gil grimaced. "Well, it's going to take a lot of work, but I'm hoping in a few weeks, I'll have an assistant to help me with it."

"And my earbud?"

Gil shook his head. "No dice. Sorry, Fish."

Fisher shrugged and said it was okay, but he looked sad about it. Of all things to be upset about, not the crash or the wrecked bike. Not the broken arm or the pain his face had to be in. He was the most upset about a pair of earbuds.

Gil reached into his back pocket and pulled out a box. "They're not the same ones, and I still expect you to take them out when you talk to me, but I didn't want you to go without." Gil glanced at me, as if he'd just realized maybe he should've asked first. As if I'd have denied Gil anything. Or Fisher, for that matter. They had a special bond that I didn't quite understand, and maybe I didn't have to. Maybe it was enough that Fisher idolized him, and Gil was soft with Fisher. Patient and kind, but with an edge to him that he used to make sure Fisher didn't get away with shit like his music-less earbuds.

It would have been easy to pass the earbuds off as something unimportant to Fisher. The way he used them was unlike how other people used them. Where most people used them for music, they'd become a sort of social shield for Fisher. And Gil saw that and respected it, even if he had drawn a boundary.

I nodded at Gil, and he handed the earbuds to Fisher, who took them with his good hand.

"After my dad signs it, will you sign my cast too?" Fisher asked. He was still pale, and his expression was tight and pinched from being in pain, but his spirits were high.

"Yeah, kid. I'll sign your cast." Gil reached out and ruffled Fisher's hair, earning him a scowl.

I couldn't take my eyes of either of them. I wanted this. Not the whole injured kid, hospital room thing, but the easy way Gil slotted into our lives. The way he liked my kid. The way he looked at me when he realized I was staring at them, not moving or breathing.

"How soon can we go home?" Gil asked. "Can't say that I'm a fan of emergency rooms."

"We're just waiting for them to have a look at the x-rays they took to make sure his arm is still in place after the cast was put on. It shouldn't be long. Thank you, by the way, for looking for him. And driving me here and getting his bike. And the earbuds and… thank you."

"It's fine, Rowan. It was no trouble." Gil was pale as a ghost, more washed-out than I'd ever seen him and I realized what it cost him to be here for Fisher and me. The scar on his face was more pronounced in the fluorescent light of the hospital and it dawned on me that I still didn't know what happened to him to cause it. Whatever it was, it had been awful, and being here with us came at cost to him.

I wanted him with me, next to me. The need I had for him in this moment was only outweighed by my conscience.

Unable to help myself, I grabbed Gil's hand and gave it a squeeze. "We'll be out soon. Would you mind pulling the car around?" I asked him, more to give him a break from the stale hospital air than anything. We had so much to talk about, like the fact that I'd gone and broken the rules and fallen in love with him. But all of that could wait until things with Fisher were settled.

Gil nodded and, to my shock, he leaned in. With his free hand, he cradled the back of my head and pulled me close. Pressing a kiss to the top of my head, he told me he'd be out front waiting.

When he left, I looked at Fisher, who grinned ear to ear.

"Don't look so smug. Gil and I still have a lot to sort out."

Fisher rolled his eyes and handed me the ear buds. "Can you open these for me?"

I tore into the box and dropped the earbuds into his

hand. With his good hand, Fisher popped them out of their case and into his ears.

"You're a menace. It's a good thing I love you," I told him, my heart rate at a normal pace for the first time since Fisher had taken off.

Fisher smiled wider. "Love you too, Dad."

CHAPTER 28
GIL

I was clammy and shaking by the time Rowan and Fisher made it out to the car. Fisher complained the whole drive back to their house about his lost earbud, about how the new ones needed to charge before he could use them, about his bike, about the awkwardness of the cast. He'd had Rowan sign it as soon as it was dry, then asked me to do the same. My name looked like a seismograph around his wrist, but he'd smiled at it just the same.

Maybe because it was so close to his dad's name.

As soon as we got back to their house, Fisher was out of the car like it was any other day, like he hadn't just given the both of us the fright of our lives.

"Hey, Fish," Rowan called out the window, waiting for his son to turn around. "Gil and I need to talk, so I'm going to his place for a bit. Will you be okay?"

Fisher mouthed the word *talk*, making questionable air quotes with his fingers, and I dreaded what the actual teenage years were going to be like for Rowan…for me.

"A bit presumptuous, don't you think?" I teased him, even as I put his car in reverse and backed out of his driveway. Fisher was safe inside the house, lights turning on as he made his way from the front door to his bedroom, no sense of the cost of electricity to be found.

"I just…I thought…" There he was again, with his pink cheeks and that nervous stammer, and I settled my hand on his thigh with a low laugh.

"I'm just giving you a hard time," I said softly.

"Oh."

"We do need to talk."

He chuckled and exhaled loudly through his nose like an annoyed little bull. "That sounds ominous."

"Does it?"

I pulled his car into my driveway and the two of us walked up to the door. Rowan was close, but not too close, and I gave in right before I got the key into the lock, taking his hand in mine and brushing a kiss across the top of his knuckles.

"It's fine, Row," I promised.

He followed me into the house and I only bothered to turn on one light, the standing lamp in the corner of the living room that cast the cozy space with a low amber glow. I gave Rowan a push down onto the cushions, went to get us water, then joined him. He was upright and fidgety, his fingers knitting together some unseen master-piece in his lap. He looked like he wanted to crawl out of his skin and the tension in his shoulders made *me* uncomfortable.

"I don't want to fuck you anymore," I said, grimacing when he winced. "I mean, I don't want to *just* fuck you. I very much want to keep fucking you. Sorry. I'm a little out of practice with this kind of thing."

Relief flooded his face and I gave him a weak smile.

"I want to more than fuck you too, Gil," he said.

"I mean I want to like…date you. I want…" The words coagulated in my throat, thick as molasses but far more bitter.

"Fisher and I are a package deal, Gil." Rowan took my hands and tangled our fingers together, turning them around until he found a comfortable way to hold me. "That hasn't changed."

"I know," I said quickly. "I want that. I want him too.'

Rowan blinked slowly, eyes turning glassy as he studied my face quietly.

"I was scared today," I told him softly, jaw tight. "When you showed up frantic about him. When I couldn't find him for you."

"Me too."

"I was scared about that, and I was jealous about the other things."

"Other things?" he asked.

"You being with other men."

Rowan huffed. "I've only been with you. I only *want* to be with you."

"You went on a date," I reminded him.

"You told me Fisher was a deal breaker," he countered, and I looked away from him, ashamed of the man I'd been weeks before.

"Kids were a hard limit for my ex and me," I explained, not wanting to talk too much about Philip, but needing him to understand. "His family was—is— extremely homophobic. Religious. Judgmental. He thought if we had kids, it would make the fact he was with a man easier for them to swallow."

"That's…" Rowan snapped his mouth closed, and I nodded in agreement.

"It's fucked," I said.

It was his turn to smile weakly.

"I never wanted to be a dad anyway, but I *really* never wanted to be a dad with him. It felt wrong to bring children into that life."

"Sounds like it, but, Gil, I'm not asking you to be Fisher's dad."

"I know, but also…it's different with him. With you. I don't know." I was fucking this all up, the words still caught in the train wreck of my throat, failing to translate from how my heart wanted them to be heard. "I want to be a good role model for him."

The tears Rowan had been holding back finally broke free, sliding down the slope of his nose toward the bow of his upper lip. He smiled at me like I'd offered him the moon, when I'd done anything but.

"You are," Rowan said. "And for me too."

"How do you figure?"

"I'm so protective of him because he's the only thing I have in this life. He's the last parts of Lisa and I did love her so much when she was alive. I love her still."

I shook free of his hands so I could reach for his face, cradling his damp jaw in my palms. I dragged my thumbs across his cheekbones, heart twisting at the watery smile he gave me.

"I wouldn't expect anything less from a man like you, Rowan."

"You've shown me how I can hold both," he said. "How to not be afraid of both."

"I love you," I blurted, before he could say anything else, before he could have the chance to say it first.

He whimpered my name and I caught it against my lips, slanting our mouths together and kissing him so he could understand how sincere my confession truly was. Rowan let out a garbled cry and grabbed my wrists, leaning into me and parting his lips wider so I could kiss him deeper…so he could kiss me back harder. It didn't take long after that for him to find his way to my lap, for him to struggle out of his pants, for me to find the bottle of lube I'd stashed in the cushions.

I stretched him while we kissed, lube pooling on my lap and probably also the upholstery, and then Rowan batted my fingers out of the way, taking my erection into his hand and sinking down low until he'd taken me all the way inside of him. Seated fully on my lap, Rowan shuddered and went still. Carefully, I petted my hands up his sides, waiting for him to adjust to the feel of me in this position, biting the inside of my cheek when he finally started to move.

"Just like that," I whispered, holding on to his waist for dear life. My legs shook violently beneath him, but he rode me like he didn't feel a thing. "I love the way you take my cock, Rowan. Like it was made for you."

"Too big for that, I think," he murmured, giving his hips a slow circle.

I pulled him down hard on my lap, impaling him deeper than his own thrusts had gotten him.

"Too big, you say?" I took control of the pace,

moving him up and down my shaft until his legs shook more than mine. "This feels just right to me, Row."

"Oh, fuck."

He grabbed his cock and stroked himself with quick twists of his wrist, the sound lost to the slapping of his ass against my thighs. I lifted off the couch to get more leverage, pumping into the tight channel of his body until I managed to get my cock to land just right against his prostate.

Rowan shouted my name, his release flying out of him with so much force, it splattered against my chin. His pleasure turned into choked-off sobs, and I kept up the same pace I'd set, even after his balls were finally emptied.

"You made a mess of me," I said, tilting my head back to give him access to my chin. "Clean me up so I can finish, Rowan. Let me taste y—"

He cut me off, a hot swipe of his tongue across my jaw and my chin, straight into my mouth. Rowan kissed me in a way he never had before, scooping his cum past my lips with a moan that vibrated all the way down to my bones. It was the taste of him that finally did me in, his eagerness to let me defile him in all the ways we'd both become so accustomed to.

I slammed into him one more time, crying out against his devious tongue as I emptied into his body. Violent bursts of cum poured out of me, one after another until my body was nothing more than sensation and need. Nothing more than an extension of Rowan, somehow living outside of his body when all I wanted was to crawl inside of his chest and live there instead.

Still lodged inside of him and not ready to leave, I

laid us down on the couch, arranging Rowan on my chest. Both of us struggled for breath, sweaty and spent, but when I searched out his mouth for another kiss, he came willingly. His lips were already wet from my spit and kiss-swollen, and I was happy to kiss him harder still.

"I love you," I told him again, long after my cock had softened and slipped out of him. He rolled onto his side, tucking himself in the small space between the couch and my ribs, sighing happily at my words.

"I love you," he finally said back to me, kissing my armpit.

I stretched my arm farther above my head and Rowan made a happy sound, snuggling closer in every way he could, taking a deep breath and kissing me there a second time and a third.

"You smell so good," he murmured.

"I smell like sex," I said. "I smell like you."

"Well, I like it," he said.

I hummed, letting my eyes fall closed as he made himself at home with me. "Just like?"

"I love it," he corrected. "I love you."

Rowan yawned, and I yawned. I gave us five more minutes, then pushed us both back into seated positions on the couch. He grumbled the whole way, shivering when he landed on my leg and my cum trickled out of his hole, dripping down the top of my thigh.

"You should get home to your son," I suggested, kissing the top of his head.

"He'll be okay awhile longer."

I exhaled into his hair, wrapping my arms around his shoulders and holding him as tight as I could without worrying about breaking his bones.

"Are you sure?" I asked.

"He's a resilient kid," Rowan said, lips stretched into a tight line, almost a frown but not quite there. "He can do a lot more on his own than I realized, I think. Or more than I wanted to admit."

"You're pretty resilient too," I said, sliding my hands down to his hips and flexing my fingers around him. "You packed up your whole life and moved into a house that needs a professional renovation crew, not a single dad with a cable subscription and a dream."

"I don't even have cable," he said.

"Even more impressive." I smiled at Rowan's softness and kissed the freckles on his cheek. His tears had long since dried, and I liked the way exhaustion looked on him.

"I'm just doing what I have to do."

"You're doing so much more than that. I see it, and Fisher does too. You've raised a good kid, Rowan. You should be proud."

"I'm too tired to be proud." He yawned and dropped his forehead against my shoulder. "I think the adrenaline from earlier is finally wearing off."

"We can go back to your house or Fisher can come over here," I said. "The choice is yours, but it's one of the two."

He grumbled, throwing himself off my lap with as much dramatics as he could muster, which was a shocking amount. I must have not fucked him well enough. I'd have to do better next time.

Which…

There would be a lot of next times, and I was so thankful for that.

Rowan loved me, and I wasn't going to lose him anymore.

I took a deep breath, my lungs rattling as they filled to the brim, but when I exhaled, all I felt was peace and belonging…the comfort of home with Rowan in my arms.

"Let's go back to mine," he said.

I helped him to his feet, helped him get dressed, sat him back down on his shaking legs while I went to pack myself an overnight bag.

"Ready, Rowan?" I asked next, hand on the door, his car keys in my hand.

He smiled up at me and took my hand.

"Ready."

CHAPTER 29
ROWAN

After all was said and done, Gil steered us both toward the bathroom, where we cleaned up and made ourselves presentable. A shower was probably a better idea, but I think Gil worried that I was at the limit of time I was willing to be away from Fisher.

I tried not to let myself think of the worst case scenario, but the thought of what could have happened to him still had me shaking. Gil gathered me into his arms from behind and kissed my neck.

"You okay?"

Yes and no. Gil loved me. My kid had gotten into an accident, wrecked his bike, lost an earbud, and broke his arm. But Gil loved me.

"It's been a long day."

He kissed my neck again, then pulled away. Reaching into a drawer, he grabbed a new toothbrush, still in the package and gave me a smile. "Okay, let's go check on the kid."

Gil tugged me out of his house and down the driveway to where my car was parked.

"Where's his bike?"

Gil shot me a look. "I brought it home and put it in the garage. Did you want to look at it?"

His brow furrowed in a way that suggested to me that maybe I didn't want to see it. At least not just yet.

"Not tonight." I needed to prepare myself to see what became of the bike. To see what could have become of my kid. Currently, I felt too fragile. Stretched too thin to handle seeing the twisted, broken, frame.

Gil drove me home and I didn't mind letting him. Usually when crises happened in my life, it was all on me to navigate them. It was all on me to look after Fisher, and myself, and everything else. But now, I had Gil.

We got out of the car and I looked at the house that had started to feel a lot more like home with Gil standing next to me, holding my hand again.

"Did I thank you for today? For looking for Fisher. For coming with me? For everything."

"You don't need to," Gil said, but he pulled me closer and dusted a kiss against my lips.

"Being in the hospital was rough for you, wasn't it?" I turned to him and traced the tip of my finger down his scar.

"It's not my favorite place to be, no."

"Thank you."

Gil smirked at me, then motioned to the front door. "Let's go see how he's holding up."

Fisher had left the door unlocked and I walked inside to find him stretched out on the couch, his arm pillowed on his chest. Now that he was sleeping, he looked so much younger. Nothing had prepared me for today. For seeing him in that hospital bed, small and pale and sad.

"I don't want to move him," I whispered to Gil.

"Would he be more comfortable in his room?"

I shook my head. "I don't think it makes a difference." Grabbing the blanket from the back of the couch, I pulled it down over my son.

I didn't think we'd been gone all that long, but Fisher had microwaved himself something to eat and drank a glass of milk. I took his dirty dishes to the kitchen.

"You've done a lot of work to this place."

Putting the dishes in the sink, I rinsed out the milk glass. "You're familiar with the house?"

"Not as such, but it fell into disrepair over the years and when it went up for sale, I took a look at the listing. You've been busy."

"Did you want the tour?" I asked him.

"Tonight you can show me your room. Tomorrow you can show me the rest."

I stopped only to get a couple of waters from the fridge before leading Gil down the hall to my room. I'd finished most of the renovations in here. The original flooring was hardwood, and though it was worn in places, I'd covered those with area rugs. I'd painted the walls a blue that was more blueberry than navy and changed out the light fixtures.

The bedding was still rumpled from last night when I'd done more tossing and turning than sleeping.

I was keenly aware of the way Gil surveyed my room. The overflowing laundry basket and messy bed. The stack of books on my nightstand. The bottle of lube I'd forgotten to put away.

My gaze slid to Gil and I watched him examine my space. It felt good having him in here, especially knowing that he was going to stay awhile. At least long enough that he needed a toothbrush.

"My bathroom is through here."

"You've done a lot." Gil sounded impressed.

"When I was a kid, my grandpa was a handyman. I spent summers working with him until he passed. A lot of the knowledge stuck."

"You continue to surprise me." Gil buried his face in the curve of my neck and was kissing me there when my phone started vibrating in my pocket. I'd intended to turn it off and ignore the world, but I saw Eric's name on the screen.

"Sorry, it's my best friend. I'll be quick."

Gil leaned against the sink. "Take your time."

"Eric, Can I——"

"What happened to Fisher?"

"What? He broke his arm, but he's fine. How do you even know?" I reached for Gil and put my hand on his arm. He surprised me by taking my hand and brushing a kiss across the back of it.

"He posted a story to his social media. Just his arm in a cast and the caption 'vibes.'"

I exhaled a sigh, the weight of the past few hours threatening to take me to my knees. Gil must have sensed it because he pulled me close and wrapped his arms around me. Was it just the emotional rollercoaster of the day that made him continually reach for me, or was that how it was going to be between us going forward. I could definitely get used to it.

"Rowan. Rowan." Eric's voice came through my stupor and I winced.

"Sorry. It's been a long day. Fisher's fine. The break was nice and clean and it should heal up with no problems."

"Yeah, but how are you? What happened?"

"He wiped out on his bike. Broke his arm, scratched his face up pretty good, but he's fine otherwise." I quelled the urge to go check on him, if only because I didn't think I could make it all the way to the living room under my own steam. The adrenaline had me feeling weak and woozy and ready for bed.

"How are you?"

"I'm okay. I've been better, but I'm okay. Fisher's fine, that's what matters. Listen, Eric, it's been a long day. I'll call you tomorrow and fill you in on everything okay?"

"You better. Tell Fisher that I'll be out to visit before that cast comes off and I expect him to save me a space to sign it."

"I will. Talk to you tomorrow."

"You better," Eric repeated as I ended the call. I turned my phone off and set it aside.

"I'm so tired." I leaned my body against Gil's, resting my head on his shoulder.

"Too tired to shower with me?" Gil skimmed his hands down my back and cupped my ass.

"Come to think of it, I do have enough energy to shower." I started to reach for my shirt, but Gil batted my hands away and took it off me. He flicked the button of my pants open and dragged them down, bending to help me take them off. On one knee, he paused and looked up at me, then leaned in and brushed a kiss against my hip.

"You're obsessed with that bit of me."

Gil dragged his fingers over my skin. "You have a cluster of freckles here. They're worth obsessing over."

He was on his feet in the next moment, caging me against the wall, my naked body pressed against his fully clothed one. Gil brushed his knuckles against my cheek, then tucked his fingers under my chin and tilted my head back.

If I hadn't already known that he loved me, the kiss would have clued me in. Gil kissed me like I was something precious. Something worth kissing. Someone he wanted to keep kissing. It was gentle, but behind the softness, there was an intensity that stole my breath.

He pulled away, leaving me feeling bereft.

"Start the shower, Rowan."

Goosebumps crawled up my arms. I did as I was told and adjusted the temperature before stepping in. I let the spray hit my chest before closing my eyes and moving forward to let it wash over my face. I held my breath for a few seconds, then turned and sucked in a deep inhale.

Gil stepped into the shower. Reaching for me, he pulled me in, gathered me close. Kissed me like it was a competition and he needed to come in first place. If I thought I was too tired to for sex, my dick had other ideas.

I let Gil crowd me against the wall. Let him devour me. I clung to him and fell deeper in love with him. I'd never stood a chance against this man. Not from that first moment in his garage when he'd won over Fisher with his patience. Or from that first kiss. Or the second. Maybe it was that all my fumbling and bumbling never seemed to diminish his opinion of me.

Maybe it was destiny.

Maybe it was just him.

When Gil wrapped his hand around our cocks, a sound tore out of me, echoing off the bathroom walls.

He reached up, covering my mouth with his other hand before giving me a heated look. His dark hair plastered down against his skin, save for the shock of white at the top of his scar.

"Quiet, Rowan."

He didn't have to tell me why.

I whimpered into the palm of his hand as he continued to jerk us off together. My hands had a mind of their own and I gently dragged my fingertips through the white strands, then down the contour of his face.

When I whimpered again, it was because my orgasm built, and built, until I thought I'd die if I didn't come.

Gil broke first, his release slamming into him. He pulled his hand away from my mouth and replaced it with his own, muffling his cries against my lips. I took them. Consumed them. And then I was coming too, moaning and writhing as he continued to stroke my cock. He kept going until I laughed and twisted my hips to try and escape him.

"Stop. I can't take anymore."

Gil rested his forehead against mine and closed his eyes. For the next few minutes, we stayed like that. Existing in a bubble of steam and post-sex haze. Then I kissed the corner of his mouth.

"Take me to bed, Gil."

"I don't think I have a third one in me." He smirked and leaned in close, stealing a kiss of his own. "Yet."

CHAPTER 30
GIL

The next morning, I woke up early with Rowan plastered against my chest and covered in sweat. Carefully, I peeled him off of me, lamenting the waste of his impressive morning erection, then I pulled on my jeans and headed to the kitchen to make coffee. I hadn't been blowing smoke the night before when I told him how impressed I was with the work he'd done on the house. He'd moved in barely more than a month ago and everything was nearly finished and new. Clearly, when he hadn't been bent over the back of my couch, he'd found more than enough ways to keep himself busy here. I was proud of the things he'd done, the man he was.

Proud to call him mine.

In the kitchen, I opened freshly painted cabinets until I found coffee and mugs, then I set a pot to brewing and turned my attention to the fridge. Rowan's fridge was much better stocked than mine because he had Fisher to feed, and for the first time since I'd confessed my feelings and my intentions for Rowan, I imagined I could get used to a life with him.

I'd just pulled a carton of eggs out of the fridge when something buzzed against my leg. Startled, I slapped my thigh, quickly realizing it was my cell phone. In all the things I grabbed at home before we left, I'd forgotten a charger. I'd forgotten about my phone entirely, evidenced by the five-percent battery life when I swiped the screen awake.

The vibration had been a message from Jack, worried that he hadn't heard from me the day before, knowing that Sunday was my quiet day and he didn't want to bother me, but…

I'm fine. Better than. Explain later.

JACK

Does this have to do with the ginger neighbor of yours?

I said later.

Zombie noises from the hallway grew louder, and then Fisher appeared in the kitchen, hair sticking up every which way and his eyes half-closed. He had the new earbuds in, and he slowly blinked me into focus.

"Are those on?" I asked.

He squinted hard and pulled one out. "What?"

"I asked if they were on."

Fisher nodded and put it back in, throwing himself down at the table, making a pillow of his good arm and dropping his head down with a thump.

"Can you still hear me?" I asked.

He nodded.

"Eggs?"

Another nod.

"Bacon?"

Negative.

"Just eggs?"

Fisher propped his chin on his cast, winced, and readjusted. "Sausage."

"I didn't see sausage," I said.

"The drawer with the meat." He put his head down again, effectively dismissing me.

I set the eggs on the counter and went back to the fridge, opening all three drawers before I found the meat drawer. I'd never had a meat drawer, and I had no frame of reference if that was a normal thing or not. Philip and I never had one, and Jack definitely didn't. But the Verne household did.

Duly noted.

It wasn't long before the kitchen filled with the smell of coffee and breakfast meat, but there was still no sign of Rowan from the bedroom. I shoved a plate of eggs and sausage against Fisher's wrist and he righted himself with a yawn.

"Do you drink coffee?" I asked him, setting my plate on the table across from him.

"Dad doesn't want me to do it too much."

"Your dad's asleep."

Fisher grinned and nodded. I slid my half-empty mug toward him and poured a fresh one for myself. I eyed him when he took his first drink of it, nose scrunching up, but he swallowed it down without a protest. We both dug into our breakfast without a word, and I was halfway through the last link of my sausage when Rowan finally appeared in the hallway. He was as wrecked from sleep as Fisher, but probably way more on the inside than he bothered to show. When he saw me sitting at the table with his son, the biggest and softest smile took up residence on his face.

"Good morning," I said, glancing up at him over the top of Fisher's head.

Fisher's eyes flashed, and he shoved his coffee toward my plate. I slid my mug to my right, and smiled back at Rowan.

"Coffee's ready."

Rowan scrubbed a hand down his face and shuffled around the table, sinking down into the seat beside me and taking the mug I'd been drinking from while his son drank from mine. I winked at Fisher, who finished off his breakfast in record time and stood with all the awkward speed of a newborn gazelle.

"Your plate," Rowan said. "Take it to the sink."

Fisher grumbled something, but did as he was told. Rowan reached over beneath the table and set his hand on the top of my thigh. It was so simple and so casual, and it had been so long since anyone had touched me that way—since I'd *allowed* anyone to touch me that way, it caught me off-guard. I stared down at the spread of his soft fingers against the dirty frayed denim of my jeans, wondering if there was truly a future for a man like him and a man like me. It would take adjusting for both of us, but if Rowan could whip this house into shape on his own, he could do the same for me.

"Uhm." Fisher cleared his throat from the sink, knocking his cast against the edge of the counter gently to get our attention.

Both of us turned to face him, Rowan still half-asleep and me once again heading toward an adrenaline crash from all the newness.

"Are you boyfriends now?" he asked.

I snorted, clenching my teeth together and throwing a sideways glance at Rowan. We'd confessed our love, but hadn't talked about being *boyfriends*. It wouldn't be the first thing we'd done out of order and I was sure it wouldn't be the last. For a supposed one-time thing, Rowan had sure managed to change my life in a thousand ways.

"Is it okay if we are?" Rowan asked back.

"I don't really care. I just want to know."

"Yeah," Rowan answered with a jerky nod. He squeezed my thigh. "We're boyfriends."

Fisher looked at his dad, looked at me.

"Cool. Is my bike here or at your house?"

I huffed half of a laugh. "I've got it in my garage."

"Can you fix it?"

I swallowed hard. "No."

His face fell.

"But you can," I said. "Once you get that cast off."

Fisher rolled his eyes at me, reached into his pocket for his phone, turned up the volume of whatever he was listening to, and walked out.

"That bordered on dad joke territory," Rowan said gently, taking his first drink of coffee. He made the same face Fisher had, and something crashed hard against my sternum.

"Do you want eggs and sausage?" I asked, shoving my chair back and stretching out my legs.

"Sure. Thanks." He waited until I was at the stove,

my back to him, before he spoke again. "Is it okay I told him we're boyfriends?"

"Aren't we?" I rolled three sausage links around the pan, listening to the casing snap and sizzle in the grease.

"We hadn't talked about that part so much." Rowan sounded terribly unsure of himself.

"Seems to me that things with us just happen whether we want them to or not." I forked the cooked breakfast sausage onto his plate, topped him off with some of the scrambled eggs from earlier, then brought his plate to the table. I sat back down beside him, nerves spiking when he turned to face me instead of his food.

"I just want to make sure you want this," he said quietly. "Want us."

"I do," I promised him, the truth of it resonating in my bones.

"It's not like dating a single man," Rowan went on. "Fisher's feelings are different. If he gets attached—"

I cut Rowan off, grabbing his face and bringing our foreheads together. He gasped, a sharp intake of breath against my lips and I dug my thumbs into his cheekbones.

"I know what I'm getting into," I said.

When Fisher had been missing, I was just as frantic as Rowan about the whole thing. I'd just held myself together better because that's what Rowan needed me to do. The thought of losing Fisher, of losing him…neither of them were an option anymore.

"Okay," Rowan agreed, blinking hard. "What now?"

"Now you eat your breakfast." I kissed him hard on the mouth, then shoved him away. "Normally Sundays are my alone-time."

"Your whole life was alone-time," he said with a laugh, digging into his eggs. He'd meant it as a joke, but it was far closer to the truth than he realized.

"I know," I said softly, barely more than a whisper.

Rowan moaned around a bite of eggs, and I shifted away from him, turning my attention to my coffee. It seemed like a safer place to be than in Rowan's astute and observant crosshairs.

"You'll have to tell me what boyfriends do," he said, a handful of bites later.

"Sorry. What?"

"You're my first," he reminded me with a sly smile. "Or did you forget?"

I leaned in close, not wanting to admit that I had, in fact, forgotten I'd been his first. Not because it wasn't important to me, but because everything about him that had come after that felt too natural to be new.

"I'll never forget how hungry your body gets for me, Rowan."

His face flushed pink, highlighting the spread of the freckles that dotted his nose and his cheeks.

"Never forget the way you moan when I eat your ass."

Rowan's fork clattered against his plate and he grabbed the edge of the table with both hands.

"Too bad your son is home, with his super human hearing, or I'd do it again right now."

"Gil," he whispered.

"I'd crawl under this table and eat you for breakfast, lunch, and dinner."

He covered his face with his hands.

"I love seeing you this way." I slid my hand around

his neck and hauled his chair toward me. He scrambled off of it, straddling me and applying *just* the right amount of pressure against my quickly thickening dick. I'd never been more glad for jeans than I was in that moment. At least the denim was trying its hardest to keep my erection at bay.

"If this is what boyfriends do, can you do it somewhere else?"

Fisher's voice from the hallway startled us both, and Rowan jumped so far off my lap I thought he was going to crash his head into the light fixture above the table.

"Fish, you've gotta stop sneaking up on us," Rowan begged.

"Do boyfriends take me out for pizza later since I—" He frowned and gave his casted arm a shake in the air.

"We can get pizza later," Rowan conceded.

"Can I skip school tomorrow?" he asked next, eyes wide and hopeful.

"No," Rowan and I both answered at the same time, which seemed to surprise all three of us.

Fisher rolled his eyes at his dad, then looked at me like I'd just told him Santa Claus wasn't real.

"I thought you were cool," he admonished me before taking a can of soda out of the fridge and leaving Rowan and me alone again in the kitchen. He took all the air in the room with him, and it had to be five full minutes before I turned to Rowan.

"Does he believe in Santa still?"

Rowan barked out a laugh, tangling his fingers through his unruly red curls and pushing them away from his face. "What?"

"Fisher, I mean."

"No, I know what you meant, and…no." He tilted his head to the side, giving me a curious look. "He hasn't for years."

"Oh." I nodded, sinking back into my chair and reaching for my coffee. It had already gone cold, and I frowned at the bitterness of it.

Rowan took the mug out of my hands and stood, kissing the top of my head before snaking around the table and making his way to the counter. He refilled both our mugs, then set mine back in front of me from behind, wrapping his arms around my shoulders so his fingers joined together over my heart.

"You have a lot to learn about teenagers," he said, kissing the top of my ear.

I sighed, leaning back against him.

"I have a lot to learn about you," I countered.

He hummed, patting my sternum with his fingertips.

"Well, if that's how you fuck a stranger, I can't wait to see what you do after we're better acquainted."

I laughed, a wheeze that turned into a hearty sound. Covering Rowan's hands with mine, I angled my face upward and kissed him until he had the answer.

CHAPTER 31
ROWAN

"Do I look okay?" Remembering Gil's fondness for my bowties, I decided to buy a new one for our first official date. It was red with little black motorcycles on it and I'd decided that it was my new favorite. But was a bowtie too dorky for a date? I didn't mind looking like a banker when I was at work, but it was a date with Gil. Something I think I'd wanted from that first time I stumbled up to his house with the worst beer on the planet.

That seemed like a whole other lifetime ago.

Fisher rolled his eyes from his perch on the couch where he sat texting his friends. The transition to a new school had agreed with him. I tried not to hover, but I had been in touch with his teachers to see how things were going for him.

"Dad, he's already your boyfriend. Or did you forget that part?"

Outside, the deep, familiar rumble of a motorcycle got my attention. The engine grew louder as it pulled into the driveway, then stopped, deafening me with the silence.

I took a deep breath and absolutely did not lose my cool at the sound of footfalls coming up the steps.

"Oh, my God, Dad, just answer the door." Fisher glanced up at me, rolled his eyes, and looked back down at his phone as Gil knocked on the door.

Taking a deep breath, I crossed the room and opened the door. Gil looked amazing. Better than. He looked like a walking wet dream dressed in his leather jacket. He had a spare jacket draped over one arm and a helmet in his other hand. Both appeared to be brand new.

"You look…" I trailed off as I struggled to get my mouth to work. "Great. You look great." I'd wanted to say fuckable. Or tell him he looked hot as hell, but Fisher was right there with his earbuds in, eavesdropping as usual.

"So do you." Gil peeked around me and looked at Fisher. "Hey, Fisher."

"Hey, Gil. When can we fix my bike?" Fisher asked every time he saw Gil now, hoping he'd change his answer.

"When the cast comes off." Gil turned his attention back to me, his eyes catching on the bowtie. "Is that new?"

I smoothed my hand down my shirt. Compared to Gil, I was overdressed. He looked like sex on legs in his jeans and leather jacket.

"Yeah. I … ah." Clearing my throat, I smoothed my hand down my chest. "It's new."

Behind me, Fisher scoffed. "Dad's been obsessing all day."

I turned to Fisher and flashed him a scowl that I didn't really mean.

"I think that's our cue to leave," Gil said. "Here, you'll need these."

After carefully setting the helmet down, Gil held the jacket and helped me slide into it.

Once it was on, Gil raked his gaze over me. "Damn."

"Damn?"

Gil grabbed the jacket and pulled me close. "I underestimated how good you'd look."

Fisher made a gagging sound behind us, which I took for approval and a sign that we needed to get our date going.

"Ogle later. Ride now."

Gil picked the helmet up and held it above my head. He stole a kiss, then gently put the helmet on. He smiled at me, then glanced back at Fisher. "We'll have our phones on if you need anything."

"I won't."

Gil grabbed my hand and tugged me out of the house. I flicked the visor up on the helmet and followed Gil to his bike. He slipped his helmet on and looked at me.

"Have you ever been on one of these?"

"Gil, I love you, but I wear bowties to work. I'm not the cool one in this relationship."

"I don't know about that. You raised a kid by yourself. You fixed this place up by yourself. You have great taste in men. Those things are pretty cool in my book."

Gil slung his leg over the bike, making it look effortless. Had I ever stopped to appreciate the sight of him on his bike? With a nod of his head, Gil motioned for me to climb on behind him.

I put my hand on his shoulder to steady myself and I slung my leg over. Once I was behind him, Gil reached down and adjusted where I put my feet.

"Hang on to me, don't lean on the curves, and tap me twice if you need me to pull over, okay?"

"I want you to know that Fisher got his bravery from his mother."

Some of Gil's face was hidden by the helmet, but I saw the way his eyes crinkled when he smiled.

"You'll be fine. I've got you."

The engine roared to life, and a thrill shot through me. Or maybe that was terror. Gil reached around and pulled my arms around his waist.

"Hang on!" He yelled over top of the rumble of the engine, and then we were off.

He started off slow, probably to ease me into the feeling of being on the back of a bike. At first, I would have been forced to admit that I was tense and terrified. But as the minutes ticked by, I got more and more comfortable behind Gil. I trusted him. I'd known it before, but I knew I'd never get on the back of just anyone's motorcycle.

After winding our way through town, Gil took us up toward the vista. The road was full of corners and I pressed myself a little tighter against him as he worked his way up to the top. Emotions I couldn't name raced through me, threatening to pull me apart.

I was giddy, I realized. Effortlessly light and free. Untouched by the stress of daily living and the worries of raising a kid and trying to keep him alive and whole and happy. And all the other things that usually weighed on me disappeared. The wind took them from me.

We came to a stop at the top of the vista and Gil turned the bike off, the sudden quiet jarring after hearing the engine for so long. Gil held the bike steady while I got off first. My legs wobbled for a brief moment before I got them under control. Gil got off the bike next and pulled his helmet from his head.

He was effortlessly sexy. Unfairly gorgeous. And I knew it bothered him sometimes, but his scar only added to his sex appeal. Which reminded me to ask about how he'd gotten it.

I pulled my helmet off and Gil took it from me, putting it with the bike.

"Aren't you going to enjoy the view?" Gil asked when he closed the distance between us and wrapped his arms around me.

"I am," I said, not looking away from him. My gaze flicked to his scar. "You never told me how you got that."

"I thought you'd never ask." But instead of answering, he just smiled at me.

"How'd you get the scar, Gil?"

"It was a motorcycle accident. It was just after my breakup with Phil, and I shouldn't have been out on it that night anyway."

"Oh, God." I felt the blood drain from my face and pool in my feet. I might have lost him before I even met him. "Aren't you worried you'll crash again?"

"That was a one-time thing. I'd been in a bad place; I don't ride when I'm worked up like that anymore."

Threading my hands through his hair, I held him

tight, staring into his eyes. "You did, though, the other night. You went looking for Fisher."

"Of course I did. Fisher's important."

"Gil ..." I had no words for him that would encompass what it meant to me for him to have done that. He'd broken his rules for me, for Fisher. He could have been hurt, or worse. My worry must have shown on my face because Gil's expression softened.

"Rowan, I'm fine. Fall down seven times, stand up eight."

"What?"

"It's an old proverb."

"Motorcycles, views of the city, and proverbs, all on a first date. How'd I get so lucky?" I leaned in, tipping my face to look up at him. "Are all your first dates like this?"

Gil scoffed. "Hardly. But I have this really great guy I'm trying to impress. Is it working?"

"I'll tell you, but it'll cost you a kiss."

Gil slanted his mouth over mine and devoured me. Wrapping an arm around my waist, he buried the other in my hair. I looped my arms around his neck and held on as he kissed the life out of me.

He pulled away suddenly, leaving me lightheaded and hard as a rock in my pants. The ride up here hadn't helped any, but that kiss sent me spiraling over the edge into dangerously horny territory.

"I'm impressed," I admitted. "But you already knew that."

Gil smirked. "I had an inkling."

We kissed again. We made out like horny teenagers who'd snuck away to be together. We kissed until the sun set the rest of the way and we were plunged into darkness. And then we might have kept kissing, but a car pulled in. Music I didn't recognize shattered the silence and Gil and I exchanged a look of pain.

"We should get going anyway." Gil led me back to the bike and waited for me to get my helmet on and settled in behind him.

I'd spent my time with Gil daydreaming about what it would be like to go on a date with him, and now that I was out with him, I wanted to be home alone with him. I liked that Gil had his own place near mine and that we could sneak over there whenever we needed some privacy. And I wanted that privacy now, but Gil took us back into town and parked at a restaurant with a neon sign that cast a pink glow into the parking lot.

It might have been our twin leather jackets, or the bad case of helmet hair I was probably sporting, but we definitely turned heads when we walked into the restaurant.

I'd never been to the place he chose before, but I liked it. It was definitely a romantic restaurant, the kind you took a date to and not your family. Gil was the perfect gentleman through dinner. It was everything I'd imagined it should be when I went out with Brian. But better, because it was real. Better because Gil reached across the table and took my hand and held it while we talked and waited for our entrees.

When our food arrived and he couldn't hold my hand, his foot slid next to mine under the table. Gil was as addicted to me as I was to him.

"Dessert?" he asked when it was clear that I was finished with my dinner.

"Dessert, yes." I replied, then I leaned in closer. "Dessert here? No."

"Oh, thank God." Gil pushed his plate away. "I love being out with you, Rowan, but I've wanted to do wonderful, awful things to you all night."

Gil paid the bill and we got back on his bike. The ride to his place was a lot faster than we'd gone before. Maybe another night when I wasn't desperate for him, I'd ask him to take me out again. I couldn't see myself ever wanting to be in control of one of these machines, but I could get used to riding behind Gil.

I could get used to doing a lot of things with Gil.

It was a wonder he'd even looked at me twice the way I'd bumbled through the first couple of times we met. The gross beer. My eternal awkwardness. It was a miracle he'd even opened the door for me.

It was a miracle he'd fallen in love with me, but falling for him had been a foregone conclusion. From the moment I laid eyes on him, I'd known that I wanted to know him. I wanted to be near him. And the more I knew, and the more I was near, the more I wanted him. There wasn't a scenario that ended with me not falling hopelessly in love with Gil Valentine.

CHAPTER 32
GIL

It had been six weeks since Rowan and I decided to be boyfriends, but calling him that felt obscenely childish in a way I'd never confess to him out loud. He liked calling me his boyfriend, and I didn't want to ruin that for him. It wasn't that I didn't want to be with him, I did…boyfriends just felt so small compared to the feelings that lived in my chest for Rowan Verne.

Rowan had taken Fisher to get his cast off, which gave me a now rare hour of peace alone in the garage. My quiet Sundays were long gone, but the tradeoff was worth it. I'd take the time when I could find it, even if it was a Friday at three in the afternoon.

I'd just picked up a wrench, ready to get to work on my Cougar again when the familiar purr of Jack's Audi rolled into my driveway. Flexing my fingers around the tool, I set it back down on the box and wiped my hands on the front of my jeans.

"I see domestication hasn't earned you clean pants

yet," he said, stepping out of the car and slamming the door behind him.

"It's just gotten Rowan dirty ones." I waggled my eyebrows, and Jack snorted in response. He walked straight into the garage, heading right for me, and I opened my arms for him before he bowled us both over the back of my toolbox. "What's wrong?"

He pressed his face into the front of my shoulder and sighed, enjoying the hug before rolling out of it and throwing himself down onto an overturned bucket.

"The wedding's tonight," he said.

I bit down hard on the inside of my cheek, a dozen different responses on the tip of my tongue, none of them the right one. "Sorry."

Jack snorted again, glancing up at me from beneath his lashes. "Why are you sorry?"

"Because he's your family. They're all your family."

He shook his head. "They didn't want him how he was. Didn't want you. And they sure as shit don't want me."

"Have you talked to your parents lately?" I leaned against the toolbox then decided better of it. I went into the house, got two beers, and came back. Jack hadn't moved, but he eyed Fisher's mangled bike, flipped upside down and resting next to my motorcycle. I handed him one of the beers and waited for him to take a drink.

"Not since I told them I wasn't going to stand up for what they were forcing on everyone. I told them how many lives they were ruining…"

"I don't know if I've told you lately, but I love you, Jack."

He squinted up at me, beer raised for a drink. "Does Rowan know?"

"Not like that, you prick." I stacked the bottom of my bottle on the top of his, clanking the glass together so his immediately began to foam over.

"You absolute piece of shit."

Jack slurped up as much of the beer as he could manage, only a few drops landing on his slacks before the contents of the bottle settled. We laughed together, and that was the last we talked about his brother and their parents. I'd long ago made peace with how things had ended between me and Philip. If anything, Rowan had unwittingly been key in that. He and Fisher had inadvertently shown me a life I never knew could be mine.

"Where's the kid?" Jack asked after he finished half his beer.

"Rowan took him to get his cast off then we're gonna start on getting his bike put back together."

Jack's mouth twitched into a smile that he hid behind the lip of the bottle. "I'll finish this and get out of your hair."

"You don't have to leave," I told him, kicking his foot. "You're family."

As if on cue, Rowan pulled into the driveway, parking next to Jack. Fisher was out of the car first, sullen as he always was, with his hood up and his earbuds in. Orange curls poked out over his forehead and he blissfully ignored whatever Rowan was saying to him.

"How's the arm?" I asked.

Fisher ignored me, and I looked to Rowan.

"How's the arm?" I asked again.

"The doctor said it looks great." Rowan navigated his

way through the garage to give me a kiss. I slid my arm around his waist and pulled him close, licking against the seam of his lips and hoping he would open.

"That's gross," Fisher grumbled.

"I agree," Jack said.

Rowan smiled against my mouth, and I licked the side of his face. That earned me a squirm and a shove until I loosened my grip around Rowan's slender waist.

"Do you remember Jack?" I asked.

Rowan's cheeks flushed. "Yeah, good to see you again."

"Same. Thanks for making an honest man out of this asshole."

"Hey!" Fisher chirped from beside his bike. "Language."

I stifled a laugh, loving the way Jack didn't know whether to be properly chastised or not.

"Even though they're clearly off, no earbuds in the garage," I said to Fisher.

He tried to protest, but thought better of it, shoving them both into the front pocket of his jeans.

"Fine."

"You have to be able to hear in here," I told him.

"I know."

"Alright. Why don't you take a look at your bike and tell me what you think is wrong with it. Where do we start?"

"Why don't you take that hood off so you can see?" Rowan suggested next, reaching over and pushing it back before Fisher had the chance.

"Why don't you go get us some more drinks?" I said

to Jack, finishing off my beer and passing him the empty bottle.

"I'm a servant now?"

"Well, you're not fixing the bike, that's for sure."

"Neither is Rowan," Jack protested.

Rowan laughed, the earlier flush on his cheeks quickly dying down. Relief washed through me. I hadn't realized how important it was to me that Jack liked him, that he liked Fisher. That the three most important people in my life got along with each other.

"I'll help you with drinks," Rowan said. "And I'll order a pizza or something."

"No olives," Fisher said.

"I know, Fish."

My best friend and my boyfriend went into the house together, leaving Fisher and me alone in the garage, as we so often were.

"Are you going to marry my dad?" he blurted, and I almost choked on my own spit.

"What?"

"Are you going to marry him?"

"We haven't talked about anything like that," I said.

But husband did sound nicer than boyfriend.

"Do you want to?"

"Fish, we haven't talked about it yet," I stressed, palms starting to sweat.

"That's not what I asked."

I arched a brow at him, but Rowan and Jack were back with beers for us and a soda for Fisher, and Fisher said no more about the whole thing. He tilted his head to the side and looked at his bike, ready to get to work.

Five hours later, Jack had gone home, Fisher was at the dining room table playing a videogame on his phone, and Rowan sagged against me like he'd just lived the longest day ever. We spent almost equal time between our houses, but only one of them was set up to give Fisher his own space and it wasn't mine. Not because he wasn't welcome, just that…Rowan and I hadn't talked about that yet.

Two houses wasn't practical forever, but things were still so new…

That was a problem for another day, a discussion for another time.

I followed Rowan down the hallway to the bathroom, pushing my way in behind him and boxing him in against the sink. I closed the door behind me and locked it, and immediately buried my face into the crook of his neck, kissing and licking his slightly salty skin.

"What are you…" he trailed off, question turning into a moan.

"Quiet, Rowan," I warned, dragging my hand up his chest, over his throat and to his mouth. "Fisher will hear you."

With my other hand, I got us both out of our pants, then spun him around so we faced each other.

"Lick it," I said, groaning when his tongue dragged across my palm.

I dropped my now wet hand down between us and covered his mouth with the other, using my knee to kick his legs open and back him against the wall. I fit both our dicks into my fist and stroked, tight and slow from root to tip. He was shorter than me in all ways, his crown pushing against the underside of my shaft in the most sensitive place, and he felt like heaven.

"God, Rowan," I whispered against his ear, "you're a dream. You're a fucking dream."

He hummed against my palm, arching into me like our bodies were made for this.

"I love it when you get hard for me. When your cock gets thick under my fingers." I shivered, tightening my grip and twisting my wrist when I reached the top of his shaft. "When you come for me."

Rowan's eyes rolled back in his head and he shuddered, a hot burst of cum splattering against my fingers. His spend was so hot, so copious, so sticky as I used it for more lube to get myself off too. I was close, so close, and I let go of his mouth, puckering his lips together with my hand and crashing our mouths together as soon as my release crested. I shot my load all over my fingers, across Rowan's stomach and chest. The convulsions were so violent I worried about hurting him, but as my senses came back to me, his moans vibrated clear as day against my lips.

"Quiet down," I whispered, kissing the corner of his mouth. "I made a mess of you."

He dipped his chin toward his chest, lashes fluttering at the sight of my cum splatter painted across his t-shirt.

"God," he murmured, sinking to his knees before I could stop him and taking my cock into his mouth. The heat of him was so shocking, and I almost cried out, getting my forearm into my mouth seconds before the sound escaped. I bit down hard, dropping my forehead against the wall and fisting Rowan's curly red hair for support.

He made quick work of lapping up the rest of the cum from my shaft, then he pulled off his shirt and used it to clean himself up. Back on his feet, Rowan blinked up at me with a sense of pride I'd never seen in him before.

"You're filthy," I told him.

"I just don't think I'll ever get enough of you."

I huffed, taking his face into my hands and staring into the depths of his gorgeous ocean-colored eyes.

"I was a fool." I kissed the tip of his nose, his mouth. "How did I ever think doing anything with you once would be enough?"

Rowan deepened the kiss, lifting onto his toes and threading his fingers into the hair that hung loose at the back of my head. Long gone was the stuttering single dad who'd never been with a man before. In his place stood a competent father, an established handyman, and the best partner I could ever ask for. Rowan Verne was an unstoppable force of nature, and I'd never met anyone willing to fight harder for the things he wanted and the people he loved.

"I don't know." He broke the kiss finally, tucking himself against my chest and sliding his arms around my waist. "But I'm glad it wasn't."

Someone—Fisher, no doubt—banging his fist on the door startled us both.

"Are you done in there?" he shouted through the door. "I have to pee."

Rowan's eyes went wide, and I covered his mouth with my hand again.

"There's a bathroom in my bedroom, Fish."

"Fine."

He shuffled down the hallway and I waited to take my hand off Rowan's mouth until I heard the door close.

"He knows we're both in here." He covered his face with his dirty shirt, groaning when cum smeared across his cheek.

"If he can deny he uses those headphones to ignore us, we can deny that we were both in the bathroom together."

I opened the door and shoved him out. "Go get a clean shirt before he's done."

"He's in your room!"

"Then you better hurry."

Rowan glared at me, then darted down the hall just as the toilet flushed.

I washed my hands and stopped when I caught my reflection in the mirror. Down the hall, Rowan and Fisher exchanged some words I couldn't make out, then they laughed and headed together down the hallway and back into the kitchen. I dried my hands and blinked hard a couple of times, realizing my scar didn't hurt, and I'd been wrong earlier.

Falling in love with Rowan Verne was absolutely a once-in-a lifetime thing.

And that made me the luckiest man in the world.

ALSO BY KATE HAWTHORNE

Trophy Doms Social Club

Humbled

Edged

Praised

Bound

Shared

Trophy Doms New York

All In

Tied Down

Cried Out

Roughed Up

Giving Consent

Worth the Risk

Worth the Wait

Worth the Fight

Worth the Chance

All in Good Time

Necessary Space

Necessary Time

Duality

Dual Destruction

Dual Surrender

Dual Defiance

Two Truths and a Lie

A Real Good Lie

A Cold Hard Truth

A Matter of Fact

Room for Love

Reckless

Heartless

Faultless

Fearless

Limitless

A Very Messy Motel Brothers Wedding

Relentless

Secrets in Edgewood

A Taste of Sin

The Cost of Desire

A Love Made Whole

Secrets in Edgewood: The Complete Series

The Lonely Hearts Stories

His Kind of Love

The Colors Between Us

Love Comes After

Until You Say Otherwise

<u>STANDALONES</u>

Rebound

One for the Road

Daybreak - Vino & Veritas

Unfettered

Dreams

A Thousand Lifetimes

<u>COLLABORATIONS</u>

With E.M. Denning

Irreplaceable

Future Fake Husband

Future Gay Boyfriend

Future Ex Enemy

With J.R. Gray

May the Best Man Win

ABOUT KATE HAWTHORNE

Kate Hawthorne is an author of character-driven LGBT romance, known for crafting emotionally intense stories with high heat and a kinky twist. Creating worlds where passion and angst collide, Kate's books bring you complex protagonists in fearless pursuit of self-exploration and happy—if not sometimes unconventional—endings for everyone.

Visit her website
http://www.katehawthornebooks.com

Sign up for Kate's newsletter
http://www.katehawthornebooks.com/extra

facebook.com/authorkatehawthorne

x.com/katewriteswords

instagram.com/kate.hawthorne

patreon.com/katehawthorne

ABOUT E.M. DENNING

EM Denning has more than twenty romance novels under her belt and has become an author you can rely on to bring you emotionally endearing, soft and fuzzy, stories. She is well known among her friends for her love of naps and sarcasm. She spends her free time reading as many romance novels as she can get her hands on.

Follow her on Facebook
Subscribe to her newsletter
Join her Facebook group Denning's Darlings

ALSO BY E.M. DENNING

Breakfast at Bennett's

The Virgin

The Jock

The Princess

The Outcast

Walking Disaster

Benji

Oliver

The Desires Series

What He Needs

What He Craves

What He Hides

What He Fears

The Desires Series: New Beginnings

What He Learns

What He Finds

What They Deserve

Do-Over

Rearranged

Rediscovered

The Trouble with Triads

Spare Room

Spare Parts

Spare Time

Upstate Education Series

Half As Much

More Than Anything

Never Enough

Learning the Ropes

Everything to Lose

Nothing to Gain

The Blackburn Brothers Duet

The Sweetest Thing

The Secret Thing

Standalones

Best Laid Plans

Murder Husbands

Lust and Longing

Love Me Gently

Accidentally August

<u>Collaborations</u>

With Kate Hawthorne

Irreplaceable

Future Fake Husband

Future Gay Boyfriend

Future Ex Enemy

Blood in the Water